Gray Skies of Dismal Dreams

A Collection of Dark Poetry, Strange Tales and Lurid Limericks

By Gerri R. Gray

A HellBound Books Publishing LLC Book
Houston TX

Gerri R. Gray

**A HellBound Books LLC
Publication**

Copyright © 2018 by HellBound Books Publishing
LLC
All Rights Reserved

Cover and art design by
Gerri R. Gray & HellBound Books Publishing LLC

**No part of this book may be reproduced, stored in a retrieval
system, or transmitted by any means, electronic, mechanical,
photocopying, recording or otherwise without written permission from
the author
This book is a work of fiction. Names, characters, places and
incidents are entirely fictitious or are used fictitiously and any
resemblance to actual persons, living or dead, events or locales is
purely coincidental.**

www.hellboundbookspublishing.com

Printed in the United States of America

Edited by Xtina Marie

Also by Gerri R. Gray:

The Amnesia Girl (HellBound Books, 2017)

Gray Skies of Dismal Dreams (HellBound Books, 2018)

The Graveyard Girls (HellBound Books, 2018)

Contributor to:

Ghost Hunting the Mohawk Valley (Black Cat Books, 2013)

Beautiful Tragedies (HellBound Books, 2017)

Demons, Devils & Denizens of Hell 2 (HellBound Books, 2017)

EconoClash Review (2018)

Deadman's Tome Cthulhu Christmas Special (2018)

Photography by Gerri R. Gray

Acknowledgements

"2000" was first published in *The Kindred Spirit* (Issue 14, Winter 1987).

"Beauty is the Beast" was first published in *Demons, Devils and Denizens of Hell, Volume 2* (HellBound Books, 2017).

"Dark Craving" was first published in *Beautiful Tragedies* (HellBound Books, 2017).

"Electric Edie" was first published in *Aquarius Anthology* (Golden Isis Press, 1986).

"The Final Toast" was first published in *Thirteen* (January 1987).

"Freaks" was first published in *The Kindred Spirit* (Issue 9, Fall 1986).

"The Green-Eyed Monster" was first published in *EconoClash Review* (2018).

"Hieroglyphic Dreams" was first published in *Thirteen* (July 1987). It was reprinted in *The Plowman* (Summer 1989).

"I am She" was first published in *New Moon Rising* (Vol. 3, No.3).

"Lonely Wednesday" was first published in *Poetry Break Magazine* (May/June 1991).

"Magnum Opus in Decay" was first published in *Poetry Quarterly* (Summer 2017).

"Mausoleum 13" was first published in *Deadman's Tome* (December 2017).

"Memento Mori (Christmas Eve)" was first published in *Beautiful Tragedies* (HellBound Books, 2017).

"The Possession" was first published in *Golden Isis* (Spring 1986). It was reprinted in the book, *Circle of Shadows* by Gerina Dunwich (Golden Isis Press, 1990).

"Premature Burial" was first published in *Golden Isis* (Fall 1980). It was reprinted (in a slightly modified version) in *Thirteen* (July 1987) and in the book, *A Witches' Guide to Ghosts and the Supernatural* by Gerina Dunwich (New Page Books, 2002).

"Priestess and Pentacle" was first published under the title "Song of Rhiannon" in *Golden Isis* (Summer 1989).

"Season of the Crone" was first published in the book, *The Pagan Book of Halloween* by Gerina Dunwich (Penguin Compass, 2000). It was reprinted in *A Witches' Halloween* (Provenance Press, 2007).

"Shadowfest" was first published in the book, *The Pagan Book of Halloween* by Gerina Dunwich (Penguin Compass, 2000). It was reprinted in the book, *A Witches' Halloween* (Provenance Press, 2007).

"Silent Stranger" was first published in *Golden Isis* (Summer 1990).

"Strangers Among Us" was first published in *Golden Isis* (Fall 1986).

"Sunday Afternoon" was first published in *Aquarius Anthology* (Golden Isis Press, 1986).

"Today I Feel" was first published in *Beautiful Tragedies* (HellBound Books, 2017).

"Woman of the Woods" was first published in *Golden Isis* (Winter 1987).

"Trees are poems the earth writes upon the sky. We fell them down and turn them into paper, that we may record our emptiness." – Kahlil Gibran (1883-1931)

GRAY SKIES OF DISMAL DREAMS

FATHER
MOTHER
GEORGE WALTER

Gerri R. Gray

Preface

Welcome to my Gray Skies of Dismal Dreams, where the days are never sunlit and blithe, and where the nights are always cold and wrapped in a winding sheet of endless nightmares. This is a collection of my poetry and short stories – all of which have been forged in the darkest recesses of my mind and soul.

Poetry has played a constant role in my life for nearly as far back as I can remember. I composed my first "real" poem while in the Fifth Grade. It was called "The Hounds of Hell" and was about the dead returning to life and clawing their way out of their graves one fateful Halloween night. I recall that my English teacher seemed to be quite taken with it; however, my classmates thought I had a rather morbid imagination. And how right they were!

Since that day, I've never really had the desire to write hearts-and-flowers poetry or upbeat short stories. Quite frankly, I don't feel that it's something I'm even capable of doing. This isn't to say that I haven't made the odd attempt. However, an idea that starts out as pleasant prose about fluffy kittens, for instance, will take a dark turn and lead me far away to some disturbing destination, like a crumbling old house where an elderly woman dies alone and is devoured by a horde of hungry cats from hell. Poems intended to be cheerful holiday rhymes recited in front of the Christmas tree transform into gift-wrapped boxes of sarcasm and poetic lamentations about being raped by Santa Claus or committing suicide with broken tree ornaments.

I just can't help myself. It's the way my mind works.

With regards to the writing of horror, my influences tend to lean towards authors such as Edgar Allan Poe, H.P. Lovecraft, Shirley Jackson, M.R. James, and Bram Stoker, just to name a handful. In my own tales of supernatural terror, I tend to combine Gothic sensibilities with a touch of gallows humor, and sometimes hidden sarcasm. I adore the absurd and the abnormal; therefore, that's what I write about. That's what I need to write about. The mainstream has never turned me on.

I hope you'll enjoy your excursion into my gloomy world of shadows. But don't expect happy endings and silver linings in the clouds that fill my gray skies. You won't find any there. But you will encounter a tapestry woven from the threads of pain, grief, sorrow, death, nightmares, and unstoppable dark forces.

With that being said, please come in and make yourself at home, as the spider once said to the fly. By the way, do you take arsenic or strychnine with your tea?

Contents

Walk on the Moon

The Weeping Rain

When Only Words Remain

White Dove

A Wind So Bitter

The Wind Whispers 'Gypsy"

Wizardborn

Woman of the Woods

2000

LURID LIMERICKS

ABOUT THE AUTHOR

ADDER'S TONGUE AND MANDRAKE

Adder's tongue and mandrake
I gather for a spell
from places dark with shadows
where only phantoms dwell.

A monstrous hand of glory
burns bright to light my path
which weaves through forests haunted
and cursed by witches' wrath,

Past graveyards long forgotten
obscured by brambles high,
with thorns that lie in wait of blood
beneath the sullen sky.

High above in twisted trees
a screech owl's eerie trill
forebodes the dreaded pale horse
that thunders down the hill.

Its riders face is hidden 'neath
a dark and flowing hood;
he nods, then waves a bony hand
and rides into the wood.

Without a salutation,
I know his name is Death;
I drop my roots and flowers
and run 'til out of breath.

Amidst a meadow's pastel hues
I fall into a sleep

from which there is no waking,
and not a soul does weep.

Adder's tongue and mandrake,
their blossoms gently wave
within the grim unloving wind
that blows across my grave.

AILUROPHOBIA

Ailurophobia – "Cat fear; a morbid dread of cats and a consciousness of their presence even when they are not around."
Webster's Universal Dictionary and Thesaurus, 1993

A storm was forming that sweltering day when Officer Rodriguez arrived at the white-clapboard house across the street from the derelict textile mill with the boarded-up windows and graffitied brick walls. With the exception of the alarming amount of rubbish that had swallowed most of the tiny front yard, and the great army of feral cats that could be seen patrolling in the overgrown garden whose flowers had long been strangled by weeds, the house was not at all unlike the other sad sagging structures that stood side-by-side along the street.

Rodriguez had been dispatched to the residence after more than one neighbor had complained of a "gut-wrenching" odor emanating from the house, which from a first impression appeared to be abandoned and unoccupied, save for the scores of mange-covered felines that peered out in silence from dark gaps in the rain-dampened clutter and watched with suspicious green eyes from paint-peeling window sills and along the edge of the roof. They emitted low rumbling growls and serpentine hissing sounds as he approached the house. *Their* house.

The neighbors were right about the overpowering stench and the officer had to restrain himself from vomiting as he climbed the rickety steps of the front porch. He knocked on the wooden door, which was partially blocked by the piles of old furniture, rusted trunks, and broken plastic crates filled with an assortment of useless junk and garbage. He waited a few moments and then pounded on the door with his fist while calling out in a loud voice, "Hello? Is there anyone home?" The door was not locked and the force of his fist upon it caused the door to swing open. The putrid stench was stronger now and nearly overpowered his senses.

He switched on his flashlight and slowly and cautiously stepped foot inside the foul darkness within. Nearly gagging from the smell of ammonia and decomposing garbage, he once again inquired if anyone was in the house and identified himself as police officer Rodriguez. He waited a few moments, listening for a reply of any kind or even perhaps a faint cry for help, but he was answered only by silence.

Like the yard and the front porch, the interior of the house was cluttered with what appeared to be decades' worth of odd accumulations, some stacked so high that they came close to touching the cracked plaster ceilings. The beam of the flashlight also revealed huge piles of feces, which covered almost every inch of the floors like a horrific carpet.

Rodriguez proceeded deeper into the depths of the house with a sick feeling beginning to gnaw at his stomach. He made his way through the mountains of old magazines, outdated telephone directories and bundles of yellowed newspapers, nearly knocking over a tower of boxes overflowing with clutter and arrived at a closed door at the far end of what had probably been at one time a hallway. The stench grew even stronger now and he could hear the sound of someone or something moving about on the other side of the door. He drew his Glock semi-automatic pistol and again called out, but no reply was forthcoming. The sound of thunder rumbled outside as he pushed open the door with his booted foot and aimed the beam of his flashlight into the dark room.

Rodriguez was far from being a rookie cop. He was a seasoned veteran who had devoted over twenty years of his life to the police force and had seen more than his share of blood and tears in the proverbial urban jungle – not only from his numerous years on the job but also from his growing up in the mean streets of the same unforgiving hellhole of a city that he now was paid to patrol. He had always considered himself to be tough and unshakable. He had seen scores of victims of accident, murders, and suicides, and he wasn't squeamish at the sight of blood. He had always prided himself on being conditioned to respond to a variety of situations and be under complete emotional control while doing so. He never once fathomed there could be an event so disturbing, a sight so horrifying, that it could unnerve a man such as himself – a man who once believed that he possessed nerves of steel. But now a cold sweat had overtaken him and his heart was pounding.

On the filthy bloodstained floor before him lay the owner of the house – or rather what was left of her. She was an elderly woman who had long ago lost her husband and, at some point, her sanity as well. She had lived in the house by herself for many years with little or no human contact, hoarding junk and living in squalor and loneliness with only feral cats to keep her company. She had recently died and the dozen or so cats that had been trapped in the closed room with her were feeding on the last scraps of flesh from her decomposing corpse, their eyes glowing eerily in the beam of the flashlight.

Driven mad with hunger, the cats all at once turned from the body of their dead mistress and lunged at Rodriguez, hooking their sharp claws into the dark blue material of his uniform and biting him with fangs that had now acquired a taste for human flesh.

The horrified police office began firing his gun at his feline attackers and using his flashlight as a club to smash in some of the cats' skulls. His mind was reeling, and he lost his footing and fell onto the widow's maggot-infested remains. The cats continued to pounce upon him and sink their little razor-like teeth into his arms and legs, growling and screeching as they tore into his flesh. He managed to return to his feet and continued shooting and frantically clubbing to save his life. He fired shot after shot, and even after the last cat lay dead on the floor and the smell of gun smoke and singed fur joined the toxic stench of death, garbage, feces, and urine, he continued shooting until the magazine of his gun was empty and clubbing at the air with his flashlight until the batteries died and he was swallowed up by the foul darkness. He then stumbled out of the house in a daze, and as a jagged bolt of lightning streaked angrily across the storming sky above the textile mill across the street, he regurgitated the coffee and doughnuts he had consumed for lunch.

* * *

"Anastasia, don't stand there daydreaming all day!" growled the balding man standing on the front porch of the old white-clapboard house. "Hurry up with your stuff before it starts to rain. Goddamn it, Anastasia!"

The golden-haired girl snapped out of her trance-like state and gasped slightly. With quickness she shifted her gaze from the strange eyes that she was sure had been staring at her from behind the cracked windowpane to the hulking form of her father standing on the dilapidated front porch. His tattooed arms were crossed and upon his face was worn a certain expression of annoyance and brewing anger, which the young girl had grown all too familiar with.

"I'm hurrying, Daddy," she replied, almost apologetically, in a timid, thirteen-year-old voice. As she neared the porch an uneasy feeling that unseen eyes were watching her grew within her and the inside of her head began to buzz in a peculiar manner. She stopped and closed her eyes for a few moments, making a silent wish for it to stop.

"Anastasia!" her father belted out in a gruff voice that was pungent with the stench of whiskey. "I mean it, young lady! Get your ass in here right now with that box of your junk or I swear to God I'll take off this belt and give you another good beating! Is that what you want?"

Anastasia Waverly opened her eyes and then quickly and obediently brought the cardboard box holding her collection of beloved teddy bears and other stuffed toy animals into the house and into her new bedroom. As she placed the box upon the old calico quilt that was draped over her bed, the buzzing in her head seemed to intensify, now mingled with bits and pieces of faint and distorted voices.

Doing her best to ignore the mounting noises within her head, she returned outside to retrieve the remainder of her possessions from the rented moving van without uttering a single word. Since her bittersweet homecoming, Anastasia had feared the return of the voices; however, this time she would not tell her father for she knew he would only send her back to that place where wire-covered windows dissected the afternoon sunlight into disjointed rays, and the dark hours were held together by the repetition of white shoes echoing dreamily down endless corridors of dismal gray.

Anastasia picked up a carton containing her desk lamp, some books, a small radio, and an old wooden picture frame that held an even older photo of her dark-haired mother, who had died in a tragic automobile accident on Anastasia's ninth birthday. While on the way to the zoo, a cat had darted out in front of the family car, which her father was driving. He swerved to avoid hitting the animal and lost control of the vehicle. The sounds of crunching metal and breaking glass filled Anastasia's ears as the car collided with a tree, killing her mother instantly. It wasn't long after that when the faceless voices began whispering things to her. At first she was convinced that her mother was speaking to her from beyond the grave, but then gradually other voices joined in and the constant distortion within her head became so severe that she had to be taken out of school and sent away to "that place."

Nearly a year had passed since the local newspaper ran the sensationalized headline: *POLICE OFFICER SHOOTS MAN-EATING CATS IN HOARDER'S HOUSE OF HORRORS*. Anastasia's father, John, kept a copy of the grisly newspaper story in his toolbox, but made it a point to keep the horrific history of the house a well-kept secret from his daughter in order to spare her any emotional disconcertion. A middle-aged building contractor who was sometimes employed and sometimes sober, he had purchased the house for a ridiculously low price at a real estate auction. His winning bid had been made with the intention of fixing up the house while living in it with his daughter and then re-selling it for a decent profit.

While Anastasia remained unaware of the past horrors connected to her new home, she nevertheless sensed there was something not quite right about the place and felt no fondness for it whatsoever. In fact, she thoroughly despised it. She found the physical condition of the building quite appalling and not at all like the pretty yellow house in which she and her parents lived happily before the accident that claimed her mother's life. The ugliness contained within the dreary interior of this new house seemed to mirror the ugliness she saw in her father's eyes ever since that bleak November afternoon when her mother's casket was lowered into the ground and a bitter cold rain fell like tears weeping from the heavens above.

The first nine days in the new house passed without incident, and then, on a Saturday evening when Anastasia was in her bedroom reading Edgar Allan Poe's, *The Black Cat*, and listening to the radio, the first taste of evil came to call. A chill that was as icy as death's grip slowly seeped into the room, drawing the girl's attention away from her book and causing hundreds of tiny goose pimples to rise up on the flesh of her arms. Her body
began to shiver and she struggled to keep her teeth from chattering. The music that was playing on the radio

began to crackle with static and fade away until the only sounds that emanated from the speaker were strange hissings and growls.

Anastasia closed her book and placed it on top of her nightstand table. She then turned the knob on her radio to locate another station, but no matter where on the dial she stopped, the sounds continued. She switched the radio off; however, not only did the hissing and the growling continue, they intensified, building up and pounding inside her head like waves crashing angrily upon the shore until her brain felt that it was being shredded into small pieces, and nausea twisted her insides. And then, something out in the hallway that had taken the form of a small dark shadow ran past the door of the girl's bedroom without producing any sound.

Filled with enough curiosity to kill a cat, Anastasia rushed out into the hallway where she glimpsed the tail end of the shadow-thing disappear through the crack of a slightly ajar door at the end of the hallway. At that very moment, the intense cold and the near-deafening noises inside her head came to a sudden end. Warmth and silence returned. She crept down the corridor until she reached the room into which the strange shadow-thing had run. She slowly pushed against the heavy, paint-peeling door, which coughed out a few stuttering creaks as it opened to reveal a room of murky darkness.

Leaving the light of the hallway behind, Anastasia cautiously entered the room and ventured deeper into the thick mass of darkness that engulfed her. She fumbled around inside of it until her hand located the hanging chain of the light fixture on the ceiling. She pulled down on it. With a click, the bulbs lit up the room and revealed the thing that lay on the floor just inches from her feet. Her heart began to pound wildly, and she stared at the thing with a mixture of horror and disbelief.

It was a wretched monstrosity of something that had once been human. Its face had been entirely eaten away, leaving only a grinning skull framed by a matted tangle of hair and dried clots of blood. What little flesh remained on its limbs and torso was greenish in color and in an advanced state of putrefaction.

Anastasia stared down at the thing. She wasn't sure if what she was seeing was real or not, so she squeezed her eyes shut several times in an attempt to make it go away. But the gruesome sight in front of her remained in place. And then a disembodied voice, like wind through dead trees in winter's bleakness, began to murmur, "Come to me, Anastasia. Stay with me, for always."

Anastasia covered her ears with her hands, but she was unable to block out the voice.

"Come to me Anastasia. Don't be afraid. Come."

And then the thing on the floor began to slowly rise up into a sitting position and it turned its head to gaze upon the trembling girl with its horrible dead eyes.

Overcome by terror, Anastasia let out a scream that echoed throughout the house and took off running as fast as her feet could carry her. She dashed down the hallway, past her bedroom where the music was once again playing on the radio, and into the small grimy kitchen, where her father sat, drinking from a half-empty bottle of whiskey.

"What the hell is going on?" John Waverly yelled, slamming his bottle down upon the table. He grabbed his hysterical daughter by her arm, stopping her in her tracks. She screamed and struggled to break free from his grip, but he held on to her tightly. "Goddamn it, Anastasia!" he growled. "What in hell's name is wrong with you?"

"I saw it! I saw it!" Anastasia screamed, pointing to the hallway with her finger. "The thing in the room at the end of the hall!"

"What thing?" he asked, shaking his head. "What the hell are you talking about, girl?"

"It was on the floor!" Anastasia cried out. Tears were drenching her cheeks. "It was dead! But it was alive too! I saw it! It's in there! Oh, Daddy! Don't let it get me! Please!"

Anastasia's father grew annoyed. "Calm down and stop all this crazy babbling of yours!" he barked. "There's nothing in that back room. You're starting to see things that aren't there again. I had a feeling you should have stayed in that place, Anastasia. Bringing you home was a bad idea."

"No, Daddy!" cried Anastasia. "This time it was real. I know it was! You have to believe me!"

"All right then, you show me this whatever-it-is that you think you saw in there," John Waverly grumbled as he dragged the terrified girl from the kitchen and down the entire length of the hall. She shrieked and struggled to break free from his grip, but he held on to her arm tightly, his strength being no match for hers. When they reached the room at the end of the hallway, he pushed the door open with his foot and shoved her inside. "Look!" his voice boomed as he pointed around the room with his hand. "There's not a goddamn thing in here except a stain on the floor that I have to sand out and that old box of junk over there that you were supposed to have hauled out to the alley for me yesterday. I can't even count on you to do something as simple as that. You're as useless as you are screwed up in that head of yours!"

The tears began to well up in Anastasia's eyes as emotions of hurt and anger clawed violently at her insides. "I hate this house and I hate you!" Anastasia blurted out at her father as she fled to the sanctuary of her bedroom. She slammed the door shut and then balled herself up in the corner and sobbed uncontrollably for almost an hour until drowsiness overcame her and she drifted off to sleep. The calm of her slumber, however, was soon bedeviled by a bizarre and disturbing nightmare of a skeletal hand bursting forth from the dirt of a grave to grab her ankle and pull her underground. It was the same dream that haunted every one of her sleeps since the automobile accident that claimed her mother's life.

Morning brought with it a dismal sky of gray. A sunny day had been forecasted by the television weatherman the night before; however, it seemed to Anastasia that the rays of the sun all too often refused to shine down upon this grimy part of the city. The gloom matched her mood as she fulfilled her promise to her father and dragged the heavy cardboard box of junk across the overgrowth of the backyard to the alley. She shut and locked the squeaky wooden gate that cried out for oil and was trudging her way back to the house when she caught sight of something out of the corner of her eye. She turned her head and spotted a cat scurrying along the top of the cinderblock wall that separated the backyard from the filthy graffiti-covered alley. Its long hair was as white as snow and contrasted with the dark red and brown bricks of the old buildings that back dropped it.

The cat paused for a moment and stared into Anastasia's eyes before leaping from the top of the wall and disappearing into the lofty blades of un-mowed grass and stinging nettles.

"Here kitty, kitty!" Anastasia called out as she searched through the high weeds of the back yard for the illusive feline. She suddenly felt a firm hand clamp down on her shoulder, which caused her to quickly spin around with a gasp. A cold chill surged through her body as her eyes beheld the sight of a black-haired man towering above her. He wore a slashed and bloodstained blue uniform like that of a police officer, and Anastasia could see that his face and hands were covered with scratches and teeth marks, and one of his eyes was nothing more than a hollow socket out of which squirming white maggots began to drop.

"Anastasia," he whispered in a monstrous voice. "They're waiting inside the walls."

Anastasia began to hyperventilate and stood frozen with fear for several moments, which felt like an eternity, before breaking free from the spell that held her captive. She let out a loud high-pitched scream and took off running back to the house. To her horror, she found that the back door would not open.

The man began to run towards her.

Anastasia frantically jiggled the knob and pulled on it again and again to open the door, but it failed to budge. The maggot-eyed man was getting closer and closer by the second.

The door became unstuck and Anastasia dashed inside the house. She quickly shut the door and locked it, and then peered out the window into the backyard. The man was nowhere to be seen. It was as if he had simply vanished into thin air. Anastasia began to wonder if she had actually seen him or had he merely been an imaginary vision? And then she again felt a firm hand clamp down on her shoulder. She let out a cry of terror, and then sighed with relief when she realized that the man standing behind her was only her father.

"Did you get rid of that box of junk?" he asked.

Anastasia fought to regain her composure. She didn't want to tell him about the man in the back yard for she knew he wouldn't believe her. "Yes, Daddy," she replied. "I put it in the alley like you asked me to."

"It's about time," grumbled her father as he started to walk away. "I'm going down to the cellar to get some work done and I don't want you bothering me."

"Yes, Daddy," said Anastasia, looking down at the floor. "I won't bother you."

After her father left the room, she hurried back to the window and pulled aside the curtain to look out. She found the maggot-eyed man waiting for her with his face pressed against the windowpane. He grinned, and a maggot dropped from his parted lips. Anastasia squeezed her eyes shut and told herself that he really wasn't there. When she re-opened her eyes, he was gone.

Downstairs in the musty confines of the cellar, John Waverly was cutting wooden baseboards with his power miter saw when he was suddenly overcome by the peculiar sensation of eyes upon his back. He turned his head to look but found no one there. He shook his head and set up another piece of wood to be cut. He was hardly a man who believed in the existence of such things as ghosts. However, shortly after moving into the old widow's house where she was devoured by her own cats, he had begun to notice cold drafts and peculiar odors that would suddenly manifest and then mysteriously vanish without explanation. There were also several times that he heard scratching sounds emanating from empty rooms, but they would always cease abruptly the moment he'd enter the room and turn on the light. He figured there were probably mice inside the walls.

Once again, the sensation of being watched washed over him, raising the hairs on his arms and the back of his neck. It was far stronger this time and filled him with a sense of uneasiness. He made an effort to ignore it and carry on with his work. However, a loud creak coming from the stairs compelled him to stop what he was doing and look over his shoulder. The unexpected sight of his daughter standing directly behind him with a wild

gleam in her eyes unnerved him. He gasped and then exhaled a sigh of exasperation. "Goddamn it, Anastasia!" he yelled. "Don't creep up on me like that! I thought I told you not to bother me while I was busy working."

"Daddy, may I please have a cat?" the girl asked, smiling sweetly and trying to sound as polite as possible. Her eyes expressed a wistful look. "Please? Please?"

"No! You may not have a cat, please, please," her father replied, imitating her in a whining nasally voice. "Now leave me the hell alone so I can get back to my work." A look of disgust contorted his sweaty unshaven face.

"Please, Daddy," Anastasia pleaded. "I promise I'll feed the cat and clean up after him and I'll never…"

"What part of 'no' don't you understand?" growled her father. "If I've told you once, I've told you a thousand times, no goddamn cats!"

"Oh please, Daddy, please! Why can't I have a cat?" Anastasia asked.

"You know damn well why not."

"No, I don't," said Anastasia with dejection. "I don't understand one little bit."

Her father bellowed with anger, "I hate cats! They're all filthy little bastards, good for nothing! I'd shoot every last one of them if I ever got the chance." Before his daughter could interject another plea, he snarled, "If it wasn't for some son of a bitch cat your mother would still be alive and maybe, just maybe, you wouldn't be the way you are."

The words were venomous and jagged and burned in Anastasia's ears until she was unable to contain her tears. "Why are you always so mean to me?" she cried. "Sometimes I wish you were the one who was dead instead of my mother!"

"You ungrateful little bitch!" her father bellowed as the back of his calloused hand slapped Anastasia across the face with such force that the girl flew backwards and landed against a bundle of baseboards leaning against a sawdust-covered workbench. He then ordered her to her room and threatened her with an even harder slap if she failed to obey him. With the palm of her hand pressed against her stinging reddening cheek, she ran up the basement stairs sobbing as the sound of the power miter saw resumed.

Anastasia dashed into her bedroom, slammed the door shut behind her, and then flung herself onto her bed. She curled herself up into a fetal position and sobbed until her teary eyes filled with redness and were stinging. Suddenly she envisioned the walls and the ceiling of the room splattered with copious amounts of blood and bits and pieces of human tissue. Red droplets oozed from the cracked plaster above and splashed upon her face and body. She wrapped her arms around her pillow and hugged it while at the same time shutting her eyes and praying for the blood to disappear. And then there came the sound of a whispering voice, and Anastasia squeezed her pillow harder and gently chanted under her breath, "Go away, go away, go away..."

The whispering was barely audible at first, but Anastasia could tell that it was the voice of a woman. She ceased her chanting and wondered if perhaps her mother was trying to return to her from beyond the grave, but as the voice grew a bit louder, it didn't sound like her mother at all. It was a much older voice and one that she had never heard before. Anastasia was unsure if the whispering she was hearing was real or just inside her head, but she listened intently, trying her hardest to decipher what it was saying to her. It gradually grew more audible and instructed her to go to the window. She was frightened to do so at first, but then gathered up her courage and crept to the window and slowly pulled back the curtain.

To Anastasia's surprise and delight, she discovered a small black kitten waiting for her on the outside ledge of the window. It looked at her with eyes that were as green as jade and emitted a tiny meow. Without hesitation, the girl lifted up the sash and picked up the kitten. She bestowed a kiss upon it and rubbed her left cheek against its silky fur.

"You heard my request, and you came to me," Anastasia said to the kitten. She spoke in a low whisper to prevent her father from overhearing her. She knew all too well if he found out she had brought a kitten into the house, he would be furious. "You're such a beautiful little thing and I know you can understand every word I'm saying to you. I'm going to name you... Avenger."

Anastasia returned to her bed and gingerly placed the kitten upon her pillow. She then laid down on her side with her face next to it and, as she lovingly stroked its fur of pitch, she noticed that the room had returned itself to normal and the bloody gore that had covered the walls and ceiling just a short while ago was now gone without a trace.

The minutes stretched into hours and Anastasia remained in her bedroom, petting and playing with her new furry companion. She ventured out to the kitchen when the coast was clear to gather up some food and a saucer of milk, which she sneaked back to her bedroom and gave to the kitten.

At the supper table that evening, not a single word was spoken between father and daughter. They both ate their meals in silence, avoiding eye contact with each other. The ticking of the clock upon the kitchen wall seemed to intensify inside Anastasia's ears until it was pounding like the thunderous heartbeat of some great monster poised to strike its prey.

After supper, John Waverly headed off to the living room with his bottle of whiskey in hand and switched on the television to a pro-wrestling match. Anastasia washed the dishes as quickly as possible and then returned to the sanctum of her bedroom, where Avenger greeted her with a loving purr.

"I love you, " she said to the kitten as she cuddled it in her arms like a baby. "I won't let anybody ever hurt you. I promise."

She then placed Avenger on the pillow next to her face and stroked its shiny black fur. The gentle purring it resounded sounded like music to Anastasia. The sound made her temporarily take her mind off the cruelty of her father, who was in the other room slowly getting intoxicated, and the dreadful run-down house that he had brought her to. The purring continued on and on like a tiny vibrating motor, lulling Anastasia to sleep.

Shortly after the clock chimed the first quarter of the midnight hour, Anastasia awoke in the darkness from her usual nightmare. Her body was drenched in a cold sweat and her heart was pounding. She reached underneath her pillow for her flashlight, turned it on, and was relieved to find Avenger still on her pillow, fast asleep. Just then, one of the floorboards in her bedroom emitted a creak and Anastasia could make out the silhouette of something moving in the cloak of blackness that had draped her room. She turned the flashlight in the direction of the sound and felt an unparalleled horror race through her body like an icy chill when the hazy beam of the light illuminated the faceless and partially eaten cadaver from the room at the end of the hall. It was now in her bedroom, standing at the side of her bed. It whispered, "Anastasia, come with me."

Anastasia began to moan as if in pain as the hideous thing extended its rotting limb and then its bony hand clamped around her slender wrist. She accidentally dropped the flashlight, which returned the room to total darkness, and began screaming while trying to free herself from the dead thing's cold and horrible grasp.

"Leave me alone!" Anastasia screamed. "Let go of me! I don't want to be dead like you!"

She heard her father bellow from the living room, "What the hell is going on in there?" She then heard footsteps coming down the hallway. They grew louder as they approached her bedroom door. And then, all at once, the dreadful dead thing that had been holding onto her wrist disappeared.

"Anastasia!" her father yelled from the other side of her door. "Who are you talking to in there?"

"It was just a bad dream, Daddy," Anastasia called out as she hurried to hide Avenger underneath her calico quilt. "Everything's okay now."

The bedroom door flew open and John Waverly staggered in and switched on the light. His whiskey bottle, which was almost empty now, was still in his hand. He gazed around the room and then stared at his daughter with his drooping bloodshot eyes. "What's going on in here?" he asked, slurring some of his words.

"Nothing," Anastasia replied, trying her best to appear unruffled. With one hand, she held on to the kitten, which was struggling to emerge from the confines of the heavy coverlet. "It was just another one of those nightmares, that's all."

The inebriated man took a swig of whiskey from the bottle and then wiped the wetness from his lips with the back of his shirtsleeve. "I was gonna tell you in the morning, but I might as well say it now. I made a decision where you're concerned," he stated bluntly. "You haven't been acting right since you come back home, and I just can't take any more of it, you hear me? It was a mistake for them to let you out… a big mistake! Those goddamn shrinks should have kept you locked up... in that place."

Anastasia felt her body begin to tremble. "What are you saying, Daddy?"

The man took another swig from his bottle. "I'm saying that you need to go back to the sanitarium. Maybe they can do something for you. I sure the hell can't!"

"But, Daddy," cried Anastasia with tears welling up in her eyes. However, before she could utter another word, her father interjected.

"Don't 'but Daddy' me," he snapped. "It's not going to work this time, Anastasia. I've made up my mind about it. You're going back whether you like it or not, and that's all there is to it."

Silence fell over the room for a moment and then Avenger let out a succession of tiny meows from underneath the quilt. Anastasia's face went pale as her father's reddened with anger.

"Did I just hear a goddamn cat in this room?" he growled.

Anastasia quickly shook her head from side to side with a look of fear in her eyes.

"Don't you lie to me, young lady! I told you I won't have a goddamn cat in this house and I meant it. Now where is the little bastard? You'd better tell me!"

Avenger let out another round of panic-stricken meows, and John Waverly rushed over to his daughter's bed and yanked down the covers, revealing the tiny black kitten. His daughter shrieked out a long cry of "no!" as he snatched up the kitten by the scruff of its neck and gazed upon it with a look of contempt. "I knew it!" he shouted. "Well, I'm going to put an end to this crap right now!"

"What are you going to do to my kitten?" asked Anastasia, tearfully. "Don't hurt him, Daddy. Please! He hasn't done anything bad to you."

"I'm going to do to this furry little sack of shit what I should have done to you when you were born," her father replied as he staggered from the bedroom with the kitten in one hand and his beloved bottle of whiskey in the other.

Anastasia leapt out of bed and followed her father down the hallway and into the bathroom. He placed the bottle on top of the toilet tank and then, with his free hand, lifted up the hard plastic lid of pink. He proceeded to drop the helpless kitten into the toilet bowl, and it immediately cried out and hissed and thrashed about in a desperate attempt to escape from the cold water. Anastasia let out a horror-stricken scream as she witnessed her father crouch down and, with both of his hands, hold the struggling kitten under the water in an attempt to drown it.

"Don't you dare hurt him!" she screamed; her eyes growing wild and glazed over. "You're nothing but a monster! Let him live! I'm warning you!"

She picked up the whiskey bottle and swung it at the back of her father's head with all her might. It produced a loud thud as it made impact, and with a dazed look in his eyes, the intoxicated man lurched forward, releasing his grip on the fighting feline, and crashed into the toilet before landing on his side on the black and white honeycomb of the hexagon ceramic tiles that covered the bathroom floor. Avenger sprung from the toilet bowl with a splash of water and then took off running until he was out of sight. Some of the droplets hit Anastasia's face and mingled with her tears.

"Avenger!" Anastasia called out as she took off to search for the terrified kitten, but she was stopped dead in her tracks by the sight of the door at the end of the hallway beginning to open. She squeezed her eyes shut as tightly as possible. "If this is a dream," she said, "please, God, let me wake up. Don't let me die."

"You rotten little bitch!" a groggy and inhumane voice barked from behind her.

Anastasia turned around to find her father standing there, tottering, with his brown leather belt in his hand. The top part of his shirt was soaked with blood.

"It's time I taught you a good lesson," he growled in an ominous tone. "One you'll never ever forget!"

The teenage girl cried out in pain as the leather strap stung her and caused bright red lash marks to welt up on her flesh. The whipping sent her crumpling to the floor of the hallway. She attempted to shield her face with her arms as blow after blow from the belt was delivered to her with drunken rage.

By this time, the door at the end of the hallway stood wide open and from the blackness behind it emerged dozens of small dark creatures made of shadow. They moved with great speed down the dimly lit passageway and then took on the form of large cats – some black, some white, some tan. There were cats with tiger-like stripes, some with calico markings. There were shorthaired cats, longhaired cats, ginger tabbies, Persians, Siamese, and tuxedo cats. They emitted howls and screeches that were as terrifying as they were ear-piercing as they pounced upon John Waverly, ripping at his skin with their razor-like claws and sinking their sharp teeth into his flesh. He dropped his belt and fell to the floor, waving his arms and screaming, "Anastasia! For the love of God, help me!"

The demon cats were unrelenting and continued slashing and biting until the screaming and struggling of their victim ceased and he lay lifeless in a pool of his own blood. They then began to feast upon his corpse, ripping his flesh from his bones with their little fangs and devouring him, piece by piece, with ravenous appetites.

Avenger reappeared and lapped up some of the blood that was spreading across the floor of the hallway. After it had its fill, the kitten licked its chops with its little pink tongue, and then jumped into Anastasia's lap, purring softly.

Anastasia smiled and stroked the kitten's silky black fur as her father's blood inched closer to where she sat. "Good kitty," she said, enraptured.

THE END

APATHETICALLY YOURS

I gave to you my heart in words,
inscribed on secret bits and pieces,
consonants and vowels unveiled
like ribbon-wrapped confessions.

Between your fingertips you crushed
each one until they turned to dust,
and then into the vicious wind
you cast them out like demons.

I wept your name, I cried, I cursed,
but all the while you looked away
and gazed upon a distant star
that matched your cold indifference.

You told me once, I love you too –
a love that filled my soul with winter.
Teardrops fell and turned to dew
that clung to morning petals.

ARACHNOPHOBIA

Eight long legs of hairy horror
spinning silken traps of fate
silently in silver moonlight;
for its prey its fangs await.

Monstrous eyes that watch from high
in crooked corners, shadow-draped.
Soon my fears intensify,
for from this dread there's no escape.

Slowly it descends and creeps
across the room; my weak heart pounds.
Now from my brow a cold sweat weeps;
an atmosphere of doom abounds.

Nearer draw those legs from hell,
I try in vain to calm my breath.
Their black and tiny claws foretell
a fate far worse than death.

The evil seeps through its disguise;
I smash its body with a shoe,
and from my throat the screams arise,
unleashed by pummeled spider goo.

THE AWAKENING

In darkness it awakens
with hunger in its eyes,
soulless, fiendish, clawing its way
up to the flesh-tone surface.

It roams the barren contours
and shadowlands of night,
predatory, brutish...
its cravings must be fed.

It prowls the unlit corridors
until my room it finds.
It slithers underneath my door,
its fangs stained red with blood.

Demanding alimentation,
it finds its host and feeds,
ravenous and gluttonous,
until no more is left.

The terror of the nightmare
summits, plummets,
then dwindles away.
In darkness I awaken
with hunger in my eyes.

THE BANSHEE'S CALL

Hearken, in the distance,
beyond the bogs and
haunted woods,
a banshee's fretful wail...
resistance does no good.

Some say she is a spirit
of one who died by someone's hand,
and roams the earth
forever, presaging death
throughout the land.

Louder grows her voice of dread
that sings a deadly tune
like wind moaning at your threshold;
the end is coming soon.

Secure your windows,
bolt your doors,
and shut your eyes and ears;
the banshee's cry
will still prevail...
the shadow of death is near.

Gerri R. Gray

VINCEN

BEAUTY *IS* THE BEAST

Vanity de Milo's obsession with beauty developed as soon as she was old enough to gaze into a mirror. She had always believed that beauty was next to godliness, and that ugliness was an unpardonable sin. Therefore, not one person in her extremely small circle of extraordinarily beautiful friends were particularly surprised when she decided to open up her own beauty salon in the heart of town. Vanity de Milo was not only blessed with beauty; she lived for beauty.

A low rumble of thunder heralded an approaching storm as Vanity filed her sculptured nails and waited for her next client to enter her shop on their eternal quest for beauty. The lights flickered a few times and a hard rain began to beat against the window glass that was partially obscured by pleated pink curtains with red tassel tiebacks. Without warning, a strange uneasiness came over the beautician, and, like a dark omen, the ticking of the clock on the wall began to pound inside her head like the heartbeat of a great and hideous beast. With the tinkling of a bell, the door to the shop opened and Vanity let out a loud gasp as her eyes beheld a most grotesque sight. A feeling of queasiness began to gnaw at her stomach like a rat.

The strange straggly-haired man stood in the doorway for several moments as the lightning flashed angrily behind him and the rumble of the ensuing thunder grew in its intensity, causing the tiled floor of the beauty parlor to shudder. His frightfully disfigured face was covered in huge warts and a week's worth of graying beard stubble. His lanky body was covered from head to toe in soiled, torn clothes that were rain-soaked and forming a small puddle on the spot where he stood. Like some monstrous owl, he slowly turned his head from side to side as if checking out the interior of the beauty salon. As if satisfied to find no one else in the shop, he then focused his stare upon Vanity. His bloodshot eyes were dismal gray and speckled with black. From them, an unsettling madness seemed to emanate.

He was the most hideous man the beautician had even laid her eyes upon. His extreme ugliness represented everything in the world that she despised, and the very sight of him filled her with feelings of disgust and contempt. She feared that if he didn't leave soon, she would become violently sick to her stomach.

"I'm sorry, but I don't cater to walk-ins," Vanity said to him snobbishly from across the room, in the hopes that the man would promptly turn and leave. However, much to her dismay, he remained in his spot in front of the door, his eyes still fixed firmly upon her and growing wilder by the minute. He said nothing.

"Did you hear me?" Vanity asked loudly, a tone of irritation resonated in her voice. "I said I don't take walk-ins here. I see all clients by appointment only, and it just so happens that I'm all booked up for quite awhile. I'm afraid you'll just have to go somewhere else for a shave and haircut, or whatever it was that you came for."

The man's chapped pale lips suddenly stretched into an evil grin and the foul odor of sour wine and halitosis escaped from his mouth. The few dingy yellow teeth that he possessed were crooked and decayed. He shut the door, locked it, and then began to slowly advance toward the repulsed and terrified beautician, who yelled: "How dare you try to intimidate me! If you've come here looking for some sort of handout, you can just turn around and take your ugly face the hell out of here!"

It became apparent to Vanity de Milo that the repugnant man had no intentions of leaving the shop, and an icy cold wave of fear surged through her body. Her heart began to pound rapidly in her chest like that of a terrified sparrow just before it dies from fright. She turned and rushed over to the front counter where an ornate French-style telephone was sitting and grabbed the white and gold plastic receiver. However, before her dainty finger could dial the police, the man made a beeline for the telephone and ripped the cord from the wall. He picked up the phone and threw it to the floor with an animalistic rage, causing it to break apart. Vanity let out an ear-piercing scream as he grunted like a wild beast and stomped on the broken pieces with his foot.

"You're out of your mind!" she shrieked before making a mad dash for the door.

A bright flash of lightning illuminated the sky as Vanity's hand reached for the lock. But before she could open it and escape into the relative safety of the storm that was raging outside, she felt the man's horrible hair-covered hands grab onto her upper arms and pull her away from the door. She struggled to free herself from his grasp, but he was too powerful for her.

"Let go of me!" she screamed as another rumble of thunder sounded. "What is it that you want?" Panic was building up inside of her. Her mind was reeling. She could hardly believe that what was happening to her was real. It had to have been a nightmare.

The man still did not utter a word. Instead, he dragged Vanity, kicking and screaming, across the beauty parlor, past a row of swivel chairs with pink and white vinyl seats, and into a small, unlocked supply room, which was located at the back of the shop. He flung her like a rag doll and her body slammed into a white enameled cabinet. The doors flew open and plastic bottles containing shampoo, conditioner, toners, and crème developers toppled from the shelves and plummeted to the floor. His grubby hands viciously ripped at the screaming beautician's pink uniform, popping off some of the buttons, and he began to grunt and drool like an animal in heat.

Fighting for dear life, Vanity kicked and threw punches at her assailant, and during the course of the struggle she clawed at the man's face with her perfectly polished fingernails. To her horror, his skin ripped away like a fleshy rubber mask, revealing his true face that had been hidden underneath all this time. It was dark green in color and completely covered in reptilian scales. He hissed at her and from out of his foul-smelling mouth flicked a long skinny tongue that was forked at the end. He then emitted a strange and rapid clicking noise that was unlike anything Vanity had ever heard before and proceeded to slowly run his snakelike tongue along Vanity's cheek and across her gloss-covered lips, leaving a glistening trail of clear slime. She let out a terror-filled scream, which only afforded the beast's tongue to dart into the recesses of her mouth, where it slithered past her tongue and explored her tonsils.

The horror was too much for Vanity to bear and she plummeted straight into a state of unconsciousness. When she came to, some time later, she found that her bestial alien attacker was gone, along with all of the money in the cash register and every bit of Vanity's sanity.

She slowly rose to her feet and staggered out of the supply room and back into the beauty parlor. Her body felt oddly numb as though she were floating in a dream. She looked up at the clock; her one o'clock appointment, a snooty Mrs. Snodgrass who never tipped, was due in shortly for a shampoo and a dye job. Thunder continued to rumble as Vanity freshened herself up, fixed her hair and makeup, and changed into a clean pink smock. She gazed at her reflection in one of the mirrors and flashed it a mad grin.

Having been violated in such a violent manner and by a man of such extreme ugliness pushed Vanity over the edge. With her mind now twisted, all she could think about was committing acts of murder. Revenge would not only be sweet, it would be beautiful, she whispered to herself.

Mrs. Snodgrass arrived promptly at one o'clock. Her punctuality, as she often pointed out, was a "sign of refined character and a proper upbringing." As she removed the wet plastic rain bonnet that covered her hair, she complained: "Oh, the weather today is simply horrid! My croquet game had to be cancelled because of the rain, which has left me in a rather foul mood."

No sooner had she been wrapped in a waterproof cape and the back of her head lowered into the shampoo bowl, she emitted a condescending chuckle and remarked: "How silly of me! I don't even know why I'm discussing croquet with you. I'm sure you haven't the slightest inkling of the game. I mean, croquet has never been a pastime of the working class. They simply lack the social graces for it."

With her left hand, Vanity grabbed hold of Mrs. Snodgrass' wet hair and firmly held her head down in the sink while her other hand dipped into the pocket of her smock and retrieved a metal rattail comb.

"Ouch!" yelled an annoyed Mrs. Snodgrass. "You're pulling on my hair, you clumsy incompetent girl! Don't expect a tip from me, Miss de Milo!"

With an expression of insane glee on her face, the beautician howled out a loud and unhinged laugh and then forcefully plunged the sharp pointed handle of the comb into the right side of the woman's neck, puncturing one of her jugular veins. Mrs. Snodgrass let out a frantic scream as blood gushed forth from the stab wound like a fountain of red gore. Laughing wildly, Vanity plunged the rattail comb into the side of her client's neck, again and again, until Mrs. Snodgrass' screams turned into deathly silence and her quivering body was motionless and drained of color.

Filled with exhilaration and a strange sense of accomplishment, Vanity dragged Mrs. Snodgrass' corpse across the shop and into the supply room, where she laid it to rest underneath a shelf of neatly folded white salon towels. She then grabbed a string mop and a bucket filled with warm soapy water and proceeded to clean up the blood smeared sink and floor. After she finished with that, she washed off the blood that had splattered onto her hands and face, changed into another clean smock, and looked up at the clock. Her two o'clock appointment, elderly Miss Crabtree, would be arriving in less than fifteen minutes for a permanent wave. She sat herself down on one of the swivel chairs and waited for the old lady, with a savage hunger growing deep inside of her.

The gaudy Hawaiian-print muumuu dress and multi-colored necklace of plastic baubles worn by Miss Crabtree filled Vanity with a feeling of revulsion. "How dare she wear anything so ugly and tasteless to my distinguished salon of beauty," Vanity furiously muttered to herself underneath her breath as she eyed the slow-moving woman making her entrance. "She will pay for it with her life."

After Miss Crabtree was seated comfortably, the beautician took out a long leather belt from a drawer filled with an array of cosmetics and strapped her upper torso to the back of the chair to prevent her from moving.

"What's this all about?" Miss Crabtree inquired, her aged voice sounding quite startled. Her prune-like face bore a look of surprise.

Vanity smiled. "Nothing for you to worry yourself over, Miss Crabtree," she said in a pleasant and reassuring tone as she proceeded to tie her client's wrists to the armrests of the chair with the red tassel tiebacks she had plucked from the curtains. "This new safety procedure is simply to prevent you from falling out of the chair during your perm. I'm merely following the latest beauty industry regulations, which pertain to all senior citizen clients. We can't afford to have any personal injury lawsuits now, can we?"

"No, I suppose not," replied Miss Crabtree, sounding a bit confused as she watched Vanity securely knotting the tiebacks. She began to wiggle her fingers. "I shouldn't think this is good for one's circulation. Especially at my age."

"Relax, Miss Crabtree," said Vanity. "I'm a trained professional and I know exactly what I'm doing. You're in very good hands." She then reached into the pocket of her smock and produced a hypodermic syringe. She gazed at it longingly as she placed the tip of her thumb on the plunger.

Miss Crabtree wrinkled up her nose and squinted as she fixed her eyes upon the odd reflection of the beautician holding the hypodermic syringe in the mirror in front of her. "Oh dear!" she cried. "Is that a hypo there in your hands? Whatever is it for?"

"It's filled with ammonium thioglycolate," answered Vanity. "The chemical used for your alkaline perm. I no longer apply it externally. I've found that internal applications are much more effective and with less damage to the hair!"

Before Miss Crabtree could say a word, the needle of the syringe pierced her skin with a hot stinging sensation and Vanity pushed down on the plunger, injecting the solution into the old lady's arm. The murderous beauty peddler then took a step back and watched intently; her heart racing with anticipation. Miss Crabtree cried out in agony as the scorching chemical raced through her bloodstream and, within a matter of a few seconds, her body began to spasm most violently. Foam came from her mouth like a rabid dog and her eyeballs rolled up into her head. Her convulsions continued for just over five minutes (Vanity timed them) and then gradually came to a halt. She belched out a loud gasp, which was immediately followed by a gurgling noise, and then she was stone cold dead.

Vanity untied Miss Crabtree's restraints and dragged her lifeless body into the supply room. She laid her onto the floor, parallel to Mrs. Snodgrass, switched off the light, and locked the door behind her. She took in a deep breath and then slowly exhaled with ecstasy. Murder made her feel beautiful.

Her next client, a prissy aspiring actor and male model by the name of Mr. Limpsky, arrived just before three fifteen for a styling and a facial. He strutted like a peacock over to the chair with his nose high in the air, swept away some imaginary dust from the seat with the side of his hand, and then sat down, crossing his legs in a womanly fashion.

"I have an important audition at five today," he said in a deep, yet effeminate sounding voice, while staring at his reflection in the mirror on the wall. "I mean *très* important. Therefore, my hair has to be absolutely perfect. Not one single strand out of place. Do you understand?"

"Of course, Mr. Limpsky," said Vanity as she began clipping away at his golden highlighted shoulder-length locks. "When I get finished with you, your hair will be nothing short of a work of modern art. You won't even recognize yourself!"

The actor gave a slight grunt to indicate that he was clearly unimpressed and then buried his eyes between the glossy pages of a high fashion magazine that he had brought along with him to help pass the time.

When Vanity finished coiffuring her client's hair, she put down her comb and scissors and reached for a sixteen-ounce can of extra-hold hairspray and gave his new hairdo a quick spraying. "*Voila*!" she said, beaming with pride. "And if I do say so myself, you look absolutely fabulous!"

The aspiring actor set his magazine down onto his lap to inspect his hair in the mirror. As his eyes met his reflection, he immediately let out a horrified scream that sounded like a cow being stabbed in the ass. His fingertips touched his hideously butchered locks, which Vanity had hacked into uneven spiky clumps that resembled crabgrass. Covering his head were at least a dozen bald patches.

"My hair!" he screamed in a voice that was two keys higher than normal. "Look what you've done, you spiteful, substandard, beauty school flunky! You've destroyed my hair! It's beyond repair! You'll be hearing from my lawyer. I'm going to sue you for everything you own. You can kiss this dump of a beauty salon *au revoir*!"

The outraged actor made a move to stand up when Vanity swung the can of hairspray against the side of his head with all of her might. The force of the impact created a loud thud and left a dent in the can. He fell onto the floor in a semi-conscious daze and then Vanity continued bashing in his head with the can of hairspray, over and over, until it was battered and bloodied, and his dead body lay at her feet with fragments of his shattered skull and bits of brain matter clinging to his blood-soaked hair.

She huffed and puffed, and tiny beads of perspiration gathered on her forehead as she dragged Mr. Limpsky's dead weight along the floor en route to the supply room. She dumped his body next to those of her other two victims and then smiled with satisfaction at her gruesome handiwork. She had one more client scheduled for that afternoon.

"What on earth is that god-awful stench in here?" asked gossipmonger, Wanda Whippleby, waving her hand in front of her nose. "It smells like something died."

"Rats in the walls," Vanity replied in a nonchalant manner as she plugged in the crimping iron. "I saw one in the supply room the other day and called for an exterminator. He came and set out some rat poison for them."

"Well," began Wanda as she shut her umbrella and removed her raincoat, "by the smell of things in here, I'd say your rats took the bait."

Vanity grinned. "Yes, they did," she said, nodding her head. "All three of them."

Wanda gave the beautician a bit of a queer look and then sat down in the chair. "I've never been crimped before," she said, "but I'm anxious to try a new look. My husband and I have been invited to a party tonight at the Finklestein's and you can bet there's going to be a lot of juicy gossip flowing like wine there. Paula Finklestein is the biggest gossip this side of the Mississippi. I can hardly wait to get the latest dirt on everyone and dish some dirt too!"

She opened her mouth to laugh and, at that precise moment, Vanity de Milo thrust the end of the scorching hot crimping iron into Wanda's mouth, trapping her tongue between the heated parallel plates. A loud sizzling sound issued forth from the woman's mouth and she let out an obstructed scream and began to struggle to get out of the chair. Vanity pulled the crimping iron's electrical cord from the outlet and quickly wrapped it around the gossipmonger's throat, cutting off her oxygen. Wanda thrashed about for some time, flailing her arms, kicking her legs, and frantically twisted her head back and forth and to and fro, but Vanity vigilantly kept a tight grip on the garrote. Finally, Wanda's body went limp as the beautician's death toll climbed to four and she slumped against the back of the chair with her eyes bulging from their sockets and her crimped and blistered tongue dangling from her mouth. Minutes later, her corpse joined the others in the supply room.

And so the crazed beautician continued to exact her revenge on those who came into her shop to be preened and pampered, day after day, thinking up new and creative ways to use the beauty supplies she had at her disposal to inflict pain and death upon her unsuspecting clientele. The number of corpses in the supply room was mounting, as was the gut-wrenching smell from the rotting flesh, which she tried to mask with air fresheners and scented candles. There seemed to be no end to Vanity de Milo's cold-blooded killing spree. That is, until one afternoon when Babs McDroolson, an undercover policewoman investigating the beautician's missing clients, strolled into the beauty salon under the false pretense of a French manicure and began asking a lot of nosy questions.

"Don't you think it's a rather curious coincidence," McDroolson asked as she eyed Vanity with suspicion, "that over a dozen people in this neighborhood have mysteriously gone missing without a trace in just this past week, and every single one of them have been clients of yours?"

"Oh?" asked Vanity as she escorted the policewoman to the manicure table, avoiding eye contact with her. Her voice was emotionless and her words monotonal. "I wasn't at all aware of that. How very strange. There must be a lunatic running amuck."

"Yes," replied McDroolson, still eyeing Vanity. "There must be. But sooner or later the police will catch him… or her." Her words had an ominous ring to them.

Vanity went silent.

"If you don't mind me asking, what exactly is that room over there at the back of your salon used for?" McDroolson asked, pointing her finger towards the locked door of the supply room.

"It's just a big closet where I keep all the supplies for the beauty shop," Vanity replied. "There's nothing special about it. Why do you ask?"

"There's a very peculiar odor coming from it. Or haven't you noticed?"

"It's just a bunch of rats that ate poisoned bait," said Vanity, still avoiding eye contact, "and they died inside the walls. The exterminator said the smell could linger for months."

"Really?" asked Babs McDroolson as she started towards the supply room. "How very interesting. You wouldn't mind if I took a peek in there, would you?"

Wielding a large metal nail file with a razor-sharp edge, the bloodthirsty beautician suddenly burst into maniacal laughter and lunged at the female officer from behind, attempting to slit her throat with it. McDroolson's hand latched onto Vanity's wrist and she attempted to wrestle the file from her while delivering a swift mule kick to her shins.

"Drop the nail file, de Milo!" shouted the policewoman. "I'm an undercover police officer and you're under arrest!"

Vanity ignored McDroolson's order, and during the ensuing struggle, the sharpened nail file accidentally slashed a three-inch long gash in Vanity's cheek. A horrendous burning pain surged through the side of her face and she screamed as blood spurted from the wound, staining her pink smock and dripping onto the floor. She dropped the deadly manicure implement and pressed the palm of her hand against her cheek to quell the river of blood.

The policewoman immediately extracted a pair of handcuffs that she had hidden in her back pocket and turned to place them on Vanity's wrists. However, her feet slipped on the slick puddle of blood that covered the floor in front of her and she lost her balance and fell backwards. With a loud thud, the back of her head made a less-than-pleasurable contact with a stainless-steel shampoo bowl and she was knocked into unconsciousness.

A combination of pain and rage bubbled within Vanity like a foul and poisonous witch's brew in a cauldron. She handcuffed McDroolson's wrists together behind her back and then snatched the nail file from the floor and began plunging it multiple times into the officer's body while screaming: "Die! You ugly bitch! Die! Die! Die!"

Using the sharpened nail file and a pair of cuticle scissors, Vanity began the gruesome, albeit enjoyable, task of hacking off the policewoman's head. The entire decapitation process took her exactly twenty-five minutes (she timed it), and when she completed what she set out to do, she picked up McDroolson's head by her long hair, which was matted with blood, and shouted at it: "Ugly people don't deserve to live!" She then flung it across the beauty salon as though it were a bowling bowl and howled with laughter.

Slowly, she rose to her feet and gazed at her blood-splattered reflection in the mirror that hung on the wall. "Oh God!" she shrieked in horror. "My face! My beautiful face!"

Driven to further madness by the sight of her disfigured face, the beautician rushed to the corpse-filled supply room and retrieved an industrial-sized bottle of nail polish remover from the white enameled cabinet. With tears streaming down her cheeks, she hesitated for a moment and then proceeded to douse herself with the nail polish remover. The chemical burned as it made contact with the open wound on her cheek and tears streamed from her eyes, mixing with the blood of the beheaded policewoman. She then lit a match and smiled as the flames engulfed her with a beautiful glow.

THE END

BITTERSWEET RAPTURE

Your eyes were a hollow of endless depths
a canvas of black, where falling stars
fleetingly shimmered, then faded to death.
My soul was a whirlwind of withered leaves.

Not once from your lips came the sound of
goodbye. But I knew you were leaving me;
eyes never lie.
The bittersweet rapture of one final kiss
spoke louder than any profusion of words.

A shadow, you stoically drifted away,
becoming as one with the dark and the night.
The hands of time splintered, like fragile
enchantments, formed from the sands
of a stargazer's dreamscape.

BLACK ROSES

When endless night
devours the day
and darkness calls,
we must obey.

We kiss and take
one final breath
and dance the morbid
dance of death.

A rose of black
with blood-stained thorns
and stem so bleak
above our heads,
sings a haunted lullaby
for two just-buried newlyweds.

BLINKING LIGHTS

I was raped by the ghost of Christmas past
underneath blinking lights of blue, green, and red.
His touch was like death, but even worse...
how he merrily laughed as my innocence bled.

And his eyes were as cold as a winter's night
when icicle tears are obscuring the moon
and bleak as the peaks of frozen white...
then he drowned out my screams with his sleigh-bell
tune.

Now my Christmas is filled with wondrous things…
with pipers and drummers, birds and rings.
But my nights are all silent, like sugarplums red
wrapped in ribbons of mind-numbing dread.

BLOOD MOON RISING

When midnight stars are calling to
the moon above the haunted moors,
he lights a candelabrum blue
and turns the lock upon my door.

Phantom-like he glides across
my stony floor with velvet moss,
which leads him to my waiting bed
where cushions soft caress my head.

Fiery beasts and stormy skies
I see within his wolfen eyes.
Unbuttoning my silken gown,
my senses in his rawness drown.

A thorny rose, blood-red, he rests
upon the whiteness of my breasts.
His breath grows wild, his lust intense;
my hunger mixes with suspense.

Our bodies touch, our dance begins;
we make love in the whirling wind.
But like the dark he fades from sight
when golden beams of dawn ignite.

BRAIN PLASTIC CONTROL

My lover is a robot with mechanical hands;
his kisses are electric; he's made n Japan;
his voice is pre-recorded on magnetic tape;
he makes love when the dial is set on number 8.

His brain is operated by remote control;
his body's built with sexy silver space-age chrome;
my robot lover, how he really turns me on;
I charge him once a day and he runs all night long.

Royal blue precision metal tubing rusts;
the wires catch on fire in his engine of lust;
his brain plastic control is starting to explode;
love at fifty-thousand volts can overload!

BROKEN SPELL

Broken spell,
forgotten dreams,
shattered glass of bad luck mirrors.
Fading phantoms,
disenchantment,
darkness now where fire once burned.

Broken spell,
a charm reversed,
lost in time, adrift in space.
Circle broken,
words unspoken,
prayers and poems cast to the wind.

Broken spell,
un-granted wish,
long-forgotten incantations,
witch's knot on bloodstained altar,
tied to promises unfulfilled.

Wilted garden,
starless sky,
tears and fears turned now to ashes.
Silence calls; thy magic spell
shall be no more...
shall be no more.

CEMETERY SILENCE

Here I lie in cemetery silence,
Contemplating the mortality
   of the day
And pondering the mysteries
   well-guarded by the twilight.
Empty rooms are all that I feel.

Here I lie in cemetery silence,
Watching steadily the fibers
   slowly
     decay;
Observing all the colors fading
   into shades of gray;
Permitting present,
 future,
  past,
   to slip away at last.

Alone in cemetery silence I lay,
Dust and words are all I have left.

CIRCLES OF FIRE

Cosmic desire is burning;
circles of fire keep turning
around.

Jupiter is calling to us;
the time has come for peace and love.
In another lifetime we'll be
and in another world high above.

Constellations changing,
spirit rearranging.

The gypsy moon glows bright to guide you;
the dragon sun lights up your dreams.
Sail a starship into the center
of the galaxy
and be free.

Transcendental visions, planets in collision.
The universe is now inside you
becoming one with flesh and soul
Ride a white light into the future;
reach the other side of the black hole.

Cosmic desire is burning;
circles of fire keep turning
around.

THE CITADEL

Night unfolds with a spider's grace
  swallows the sun without a trace.
Direful in its dark enmeshing;
  nightmare towers coalescing.

Lucent phantom moon unveiling
  omens in the wind that cries.
Hearken to the banshee's wailing;
  death is in the falcon's eyes.

High she soars, then circles around
  without a fear, without a sound;
Casting shadows on the bones
  that lie beneath the tower's stones.

In its dungeon, hope imprisoned,
  stripped of power now forbidden.
Shackled and chained,
  withered and drained –
Every room a tomb of gloom.

Disillusionment surrounding,
  bittersweet decay abounding.
Silence thunders through stony walls,
  echoes in halls; the citadel
  falls.

CITY LIGHTS

The lights of the city shine so bright,
faceless people haunt the night,
trapped like a prisoner of the past;
it all seems like a dream…
time goes so fast.

Lost in the madness of the crowd,
I hear the silence roar so loud.
Shadows fill the empty space inside;
I run until there's no place to hide

Strangers turn their heads and stare;
lies and disguises everywhere.
Sidewalks leading nowhere take my feet
into the maze of never ending streets.

Look into the mirror of lost time
beyond the music and the rhyme.
Look beyond your dreams and you will find
city lights are flashing inside your mind.

THE COFFIN PARTY MIDNIGHT BALL

Come one and come all
to the coffin party midnight ball.
The night's entertainment might not be so live,
but everyone's dying for you to arrive.

They say all good things must come to an end
and no truer words have ever been spoken.
Don't bring a frown but do bring a friend.
As a rule, all the rules that you know
will be broken.

This open invitation to you I send;
except for your life you have nothing to lose.
Sooner or later we all must attend...
you can try to resist
but you cannot refuse.

No one says no; it just isn't done.
So come as you were
and join in the fun!

Your presence, my friend, is greatly desired;
Please note that no RSVP is required.

CONJURATIONS

Alluring woman of mystery,
a tempting vixen with eyes of fire,
tainted passion is her sorcery;
her kisses are your desire.

> I conjure thee of darkness,
> I conjure thee of light,
> with love entwined with magic;
> your mind is spellbound tonight.

Seductive angel, so heavenly;
she-devil of midnight lust.
Beware of her sweet bewitchery;
illusions will turn to dust.

> I conjure thee of shadows,
> I conjure thee of flames;
> your free will is yours no longer;
> your soul is now hers to claim.

Conjurations, temptations,
love is her Black Art.
Conjurations, temptations,
she will hex your heart
forever.

THE CREATRESS

A tapestry of dreams I weave...
each one a gift
   I lovingly give;
each one a lesson
   I painfully learn.

A monument of tears I sculpt...
each one begets
   a garden of pain;
each one an acid
   that through my heart burns.

An iron mask of gloom I forge...
each shade of gray
   fades into the next;
each desolation
   never adjourns.

CRIMSON SKIES

Crimson skies, like blood in my eyes,
coagulate at dawn; the sunrise cries.
Crimson skies become my disguise
when dreams born at midnight
dissolve into lies.

Crimson skies, a daily reprise
hemorrhaging above, they hypnotize.
Crimson skies bring down all my highs
when storm clouds of anguish
materialize.

Crimson skies desensitize,
they cannibalize and traumatize.
Crimson skies don't compromise;
they only foreshadow
a dreamer's demise.

CURSE OF THE BLACK WIDOW

The black widow spins her web of fate:
a silken trap perceived too late.
By maledictions from the past
is her hunger fed at last.
And as she weaves each silver strand,
the minutes fall like grains of sand.

The black widow toils throughout the night,
embroidering in the pale moonlight.
Enticing her victims with her stare,
she waits most patiently to ensnare.
Her inescapable trap constrains;
her toxic venom invades their veins.

Yet, foolishly they seek her door;
The black widow takes them evermore.

DANCE OF THE COBRA

From out of the white wicker basket
the cobra slowly raises her head.
Majestically she spreads her hood,
her eyes are transfixed and black as pitch.

Her body hypnotically dances,
enticed by the snake charmer's mystical flute,
ethereal tunes float high on the air;
her scales in the golden light glisten.

She sensuously slithers and slides;
the spectators stare and with fingers point.
She hisses, her serpent tongue flicking;
the spectators laugh and applaud.

Her movements beguile and arouse,
men gather around, but they dare not touch.
Her sideshow tricks are dazzling but few;
and repeated with each new performance.

She yearns for the desert and her freedom,
but sadly her will is no longer her own.
The snake charmer picks up his coins
from the street, and disappears into the night.

From inside the locked wicker basket
the cobra lies dreaming of vengeance so sweet
with a bite filled with venom so deadly.
I know all too well for that cobra am I.

DARK CRAVING

From my grave of wilted roses
   when the moon is waning and pale,
shall I awaken and arise,
   cloaked in midnight's veil.

To ride the wind and taste the night,
 inhale deeply the scent of the living,
And bask in death's exquisite delight,
   so cruel,
   so perfect,
   so unforgiving.

My heart beats not, but still it longs;
   my eyes weep not, but grieve in sorrow.
Shrouded dreams haunt like a ghost;
   I thirst with each tomorrow.

Upon your warmth I will hungrily feast
   and drink my fill of scarlet mirth,
'Til dreamless slumber calls with dread
   and earth once more becomes my bed.

When darkness veils the bleeding sun
   and light of day becomes forsaken,
When my flesh the shadows caress,
   again shall I awaken.

What a wicked thing forlorn,
   a morbid riddle have I become.
Suffering is my nourishment;
   for me, peace is there none.

Weep not for me
  but for thyself,
  and pray for thine own soul to save.
For all that you fear and loathe of me
  is what your secret self does crave.

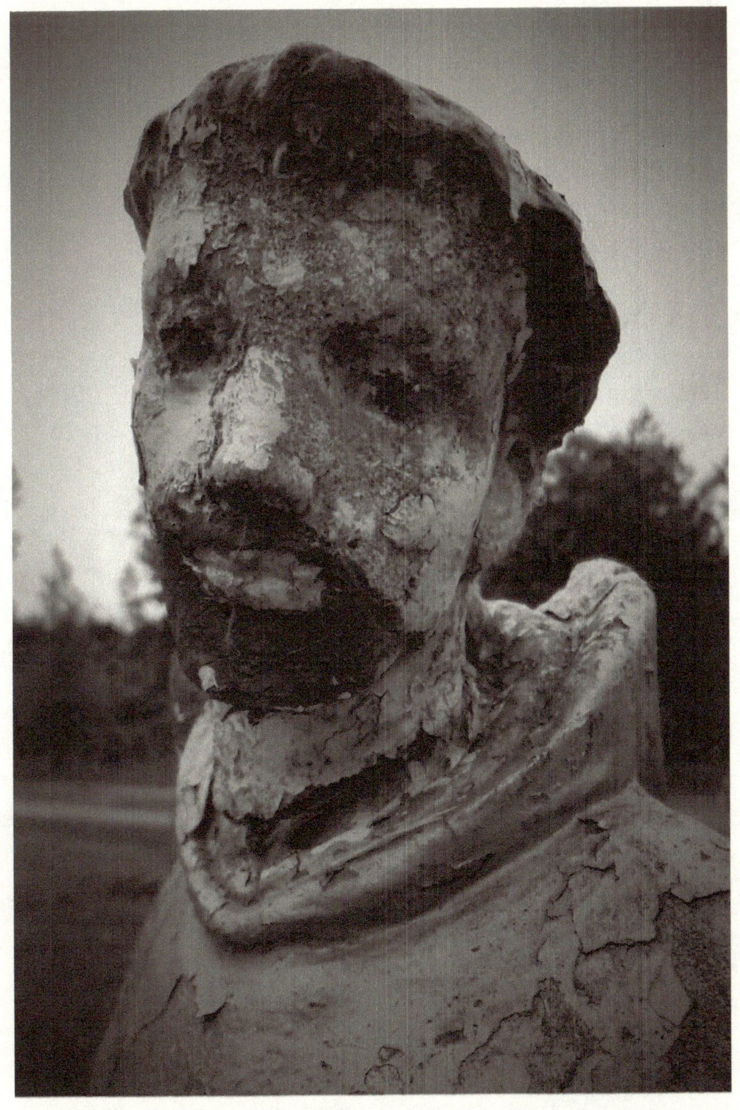

DARK DREAMS ON MOONLESS NIGHTS

Once again the black void calls,
its masking cloak of velvet falls
upon the rooftops and the walls
and deep within my soul.

A moonless night devours the sun,
a web of darkest dreams is spun.
The nightmare realm unfolds once more,
I dance with shadows on the floor;

Like cats of black on silent feet
with eyes that whisper, trick or treat,
they creep into my every cell
to weave a dark ensnaring spell.

And now within this unreal hour
I feel the nightmare beast devour
sleep so deep with thoughts unholy
'Til I wake and stumble slowly

From my bed, across the floor
and past the threshold of my door
where another dawn awaits
beyond the rusted garden gate.

THE DEAD DON'T SLEEP

Damn the night, so dark and deep,
where shadows born of nightmares creep
and cemetery angels weep,
within their graves the dead don't sleep.

Curse the day, so sharp and steep,
where specters taunt and secrets keep,
into my brain their poisons seep
and haunt me for the dead don't sleep.

Damn the lifeless eyes that peep,
the rotting fleshes in a heap,
and as ye sow, so shall ye reap,
no solace for the dead don't sleep.

DEMISE

Wilting roses in hands of stone,
weary petals sweet in their decay,
fading crimson in silence mourns
her lips, once smiling, so long, long ago.

Sad and brittle the leaves once fair,
green and graceful, withered of their charms.
Love and beauty now left to wane;
to death an offering, not refused.

DON'T GO INTO THE CELLAR!

Bryce Weldon had been chasing tornadoes with his video equipment for well over ten years. It was in his blood. The thrill he derived from observing the power and the fury of Mother Nature up close was like no other he had ever experienced. He lived every waking moment of his life for it.

The storm he had been chasing that warm afternoon in May had roared across the plains of Oklahoma, unleashing a violent category F4 tornado that cut a swath of destruction three miles long and one-quarter of a mile wide. Luckily the twister had touched down in a mostly uninhabited area, so most of the damage it caused was limited to uprooted trees, splintered fences, and knocked-over telephone poles.

However, shortly after turning off the main highway onto a dusty county road in an attempt to follow the storm as it moved to the northeast, Bryce noticed there was an old farmhouse up ahead that appeared to have taken a direct hit from the angry whirling winds of the tornado. As he drove closer to it, he could see that most of the roof had been ripped away and the south side of the structure had collapsed inward. Strewn around what was left of the building were piles of rubble containing boards, the remnants of smashed furniture, chunks of plaster, and twisted pieces of metal. Clinging to downed tree branches were bits of yellow fiberglass insulation that waved in the humid breeze.

Bryce turned his truck into the gravel driveway and turned off the ignition. "Holy shit!" he said out loud to himself as he surveyed the damage. Being the Good Samaritan that he was, he felt it was his duty to check for any survivors and render his assistance if help was needed. He climbed out of his vehicle with his military grade LED flashlight in hand and proceeded to the farmhouse.

"Hello?" he called out in a loud voice. "Is anyone in there?" Can you hear me? Hello?" He waited a moment, listening for a reply or for any other sound from within the destroyed building or from underneath the debris that surrounded it, but he heard nothing. He walked around to the rear of the house, carefully navigating through the wreckage, and once again shouted, "Hello? Is there anybody in this house? Hello?"

This time a faint voice answered him. It was the voice of a woman. She sounded most terrified and began to beg for help. "I'm down in the cellar!" she yelled. "I'm trapped and I can't get out! Please help me! Oh hurry! Please!"

"Hang on! I'm going to get you out of there as soon as I can!" Bryce shouted to her as he climbed over the debris. As he made his way towards the rear entrance of the house as quickly as he could, he saw that the tornado had ripped the door from its hinges. The woman's cries grew louder the nearer he got.

Once inside the house, the tornado chaser cleared away the debris that blocked his path and followed the sound of the woman's voice until he was able to locate the door leading to the cellar. To his dismay, he found that it was either locked or jammed and would not budge. Using a front kick, he drove the heel of his foot into the door just below the doorknob. On the third try he was able to break down the door, and he rushed down the stairs.

Shining his flashlight into the cellar, Bryce was startled to see the body of a heavyset man in denim overalls lying on the floor partially covered by timber from the floor above that had caved in. He appeared to be dead. But even more startling was the sight of a beautiful young woman standing in the corner with her arms straight up and her wrists handcuffed to an overhead water pipe.

"Jesus H. Christ!" were the words that rolled off of Bryce's tongue. Never before in all his years of storm chasing had he ever encountered a scene so strange.

"Oh, thank goodness you've come!" said the woman as tears streamed down her pallid face. "I thought I was going to starve to death."

"What on earth is going on here?" Bryce asked. He motioned with his head in the direction of the man on the floor. "Did that guy over there do this to you?"

"Yes!" cried the woman. "He's insane! He's had me chained down here for weeks, maybe months. I don't know how long it's been. It feels like an eternity! Oh, I'm so afraid. Help me, please! He has the key to the handcuffs on a key chain in the back pocket of his pants. Hurry, please!"

"Now don't you worry, Miss. You're safe now," said Bryce as he climbed over the rubble and approached the man on the floor. "I'll have you down from there in just a minute. There's no need for you to be afraid any longer. He can't hurt you any more."

The enslaved woman began to sob with joy. Strands of her long black hair clung to her cheeks, which were moist with tears, and a feeble smile manifested on her parched and nearly colorless lips. "Oh thank heavens!" she exclaimed with exuberance in her voice. "My prayers have finally been answered!"

Bryce crouched down and as he slipped his hand into the man's pocket to retrieve the keys to the handcuffs, the man in the overalls began to stir and emitted a groan.

The woman shrieked, "Oh my god, he's alive! Hurry and get me down from here before he comes to! He's dangerous! He'll murder both of us!"

With the key chain in hand, Bryce rushed back to the woman and attempted to unlock the handcuffs, but the first of the two dozen keys that hung on the ring didn't work. He tried the next one, but that also failed to unlock them.

"What are you doing?" shouted the man on the floor as he regained consciousness. His deep voice was like gravel and filled with rage. "Get the hell away from that woman! You hear me, son? She don't belong to you!"

"Look out!" the woman screamed. "He's got a weapon! He's crazy!"

Bryce turned around to discover that the man in overalls had picked himself up off the floor and was now stumbling towards him, slashing the air with a camouflage-handled buck knife that he had plucked from his mud-encrusted work boot. "I'll take your life before I let you release her into the world!" he shouted insanely. "Don't you understand, son? I'm doin' the Lord's work!"

With his adrenaline pumping, Bryce swung his heavy flashlight at the man's head, striking him on his left temple. The blow produced a gash that immediately began to spurt blood, and the heavyset man let go of the knife and collapsed in a heap onto the floor. Bryce wasn't sure if the attacker was dead or merely unconscious, but that was of no concern to him at this point. All he could think about was freeing the victim and safely getting her out of the destroyed and unstable structure as quickly as possible. He wiped the sweat away from his brow and then returned to where she stood helplessly and continued trying the keys until he finally found the one that fit the lock on the handcuffs.

With her wrists free at last, the woman breathed a sigh of relief and threw her arms around Bryce, expressing her undying gratitude to him for rescuing her from the clutches of the deranged madman. "You saved my life," she said. "How can I ever repay you?"

Bryce returned the embrace, pleased with his good deed for the day. He was basking in the glowing feeling of being a hero when all of a sudden he felt something sharp pierce the side of his neck. His mind reeled with confusion and a wave of dizziness surged through his head. And then everything went black.

The woman retracted her fangs from Bryce's neck and licked away the fresh blood from her lips as his limp body fell to the cellar floor, twitching with violent spasms. Feeling replenished, she grinned as she looked down at the storm chaser. She then let out a laugh and asked him, "Will everlasting life do?"

THE END

THE DREAM-CAT

When nighttime spins her darkened web
and silence chants her charmed refrain,
the dream-cat comes on soundless paws
with enigmatic eyes.

Her shadow prowls the fog-laced hills
where wizards dwell and magic thrives.
Windswept omens does she bring
to those versed in her ways.

She tiptoes 'round my sleeping head,
against my cheeks her whiskers brush.
Her purrs, like velvet, cast a spell
that opens doors unknown.

Her sphinx-like contours whisper of
a thousand ancient gods divine.
Surrender to her mystic gaze...
behold another world.

THE DREAMING DEAD

Rays of sun her halo makes
when hazy afternoons awake
to laughing crows and drone of bees
and lazy shadows cast by trees.

When the web of night is spun
and orange light of day is done
the starry sky becomes her gown,
light as whispers, soft as down.

Dew-kissed lawns caress her feet
moon flowers bloom, ghost-white and sweet
and crickets charm the moon agleam;
I wonder if the dead still dream.

Gerri R. Gray

THE DYING TREE

Gather round the dying tree
adorned with lights and glittering things
like lipstick on a rotting corpse
that whispers Merry Christmas.

Empty boxes, broken gifts,
strangled by ribbons green and red
fill my heart with dread and holly;
visions of dead things dance in my head.

Sleigh bells slaying, carols playing,
meaningless greetings from friends now strangers;
sugar plum lies blind children's eyes
while plastic babes lie in their mangers.

So gather 'round the dying tree
adorned with lights and glittering things
that hide the horrors of the night
and make the Yuletide bright.

Three special gifts to you from me
I give with love rejoicing...
a tattered stocking filled with tears,
the passing of another year,
a toast to Father Christmas with a
cup of poisoned cheer.

EIGHT YEARS LATER

Nights are the blackest and coldest of all
when gone is the one whose name you call
to fill your sleep with roses red,
the emptiness makes you ache to be dead.

Mornings are dismal and bleak as a grave
when far is the one whose love you crave
but not as bleak, nor cursed with rue
as thoughts of tomorrows spent without you.

ELECTRIC EDIE

Electric Edie with painted eyes,
electric tears of glitter dust she cries.
Living at the speed of light,
an underground princess
with hair of silver-white.
A poor little rich girl fantasy,
a psychedelic flower dancing free...

A superstar of the neon lights.

Hiding from the madness
  of publicity;
Tearing apart her mind
  to find reality.
Lost in repetitious
  echoes of infinity.

Electric Edie, her soul is on fire
tripping and flying
higher and higher she dared.
Touching the sky like a gilded bird,
she cried for help
but no one heard
or cared...

A shooting star in the dead of night.

Watch her ride in her limousine;
a fading smile in a magazine
is all she left behind.

EPITAPH FOR A DREAM

In the earth beneath this weathered stone
Here lie the ashes of a dream,
A dream that was forged in blood and bone
But never saw the sunlight's gleam.
In this grave lies a dream unborn,
It can never return, and the angels mourn.
It rests in pieces, but not in peace,
The sorrow death brings will never cease.
For every dream that it enslaved...
This epitaph shall be engraved.

EXQUISITE ALCHEMY

His eyes are most caliginous,
haunting as a moonless night.
Seductive,
Horizonless, strange as hell,
his gaze, like a flame,
mesmerizes.

Like a gypsy moth, I'm drawn,
unable to resist, despite
my burning wings.
The deeper I look within,
more secrets there are to find.

Inside him, there is a spirit
intrinsic and untamed by time.
His touch is like spellbinding
quicksilver moonrise.

He makes me ache for more.

In dark storms he stands
on flowering hilltops
scented with jasmine, sweet
with rain-steeped myrrh,
profoundly conjuring
an exquisite alchemy.

Chanting, he burns his candles
to ambiguous gods above.
Inscrutable, erogenous,
he ignites fires

inside my mind.

I blaze with fervor.
I crave with hunger.
I love him as I have loved
no other.

THE FATHER

With his eyes locked between
the pages of a book
and his lips wrapped around the bit
of his pipe,
he looks up every now and then
to scowl
and hurl daggers in my direction.

His joy is my suffering.
His hatred unwavering.

In his silence he dwells;
his disdain for me increases.
In his eyes swim his bitterness
and his urge to dismantle me.

Day after day,
he shatters my spirit, diseases
my mind.
Night after night.
he poisons my sleep with dreams
wrapped in dread.

I stick silver pins in his image
to make him disappear,
but still he remains,
forever haunting the dungeon
he designed and constructed

around my soul.

He sits and reads
as the Sunday morning sunlight
filters through the green
of vertical blinds.
His snowy thinning hair
adds more years to his age.
His face, pale and gaunt
like an unearthed corpse,
contorts with a sneer.
He looks away, disgusted,
seething,
regretting his vows.

THE FATHER (continued)

I picture him deceased
and that helps suppress my pain.
I nail his casket shut and then
secure it with a chain to keep him
from ever rising up again.

But he always returns;
he refuses to die,
even though in his heart
he's already dead.

THE FINAL TOAST

Gather on this black-draped night
and let the final toast begin.
Family, friends, and foes alike,
The door is open, do come in.

Enter if your soul does dare
where mirth and merriment abound.
The Dance of Death unites us all
around my burial mound.

Feast until your bellies ache
and fill your glasses to their brim.
To kisses born in flames awake;
don't let the mood grow grim.

A toast to darkness now unending
filled with hellbound souls descending.
Drink to shadows drenched with dread:
a toast to the undead!

Sip my spirit and taste my blood,
a nectar so divine.
Quaff me in your silver goblet,
sweet like elderberry wine.

FIVE O'CLOCK FEAR

Five o'clock fear creeps slowly
like a Cadillac of funeral black,
while afternoon haze slips dreamily
through slats of Venetian blinds,
falling gently on bandaged legs and
crocheted doilies, half-completed.

Aged hands, pale and faintly sweet,
touch my cheeks as if to absorb
some childhood magic. Eyes of blue
speckled with pain, watch the world
from a wing-back chair with thread-worn
arms. Speaking without words;
smiling without joy; even then, I knew.

Shadows converge 'neath attic cobwebs
haunted by ghosts trapped in boxes
full with remnants of long ago lives.

For some odd reason I remember
the silverfish in the pantry, the white
ceramic tiles that back-dropped your
agony, the black rotary telephone that
sat in silence after the doctor was called.

I remember a November tasting of tears
and flurries on my tongue, the smell of
rubbing alcohol fading from my nostrils,
and the five o'clock fear that always
imprinted itself in the lines
upon your face.

FLY AWAY, MY RAVEN BLACK

Fly away, my raven black
into the dark and bittersweet
that whispers like a velvet night;
unfold your wings and fly.

Fly away, so far away
beyond this wretched world forlorn
of time and tears synonymous;
unfold your wings and fly.

Fly away, my raven black
into a dream of indigo.
No silent tomb nor cobwebbed gloom
will be your gilded cage.

Fly away, so far away
beyond the fading twilight mist.
Embrace the freedom of the sky;
unfold your wings and fly.

FOR A MOMENT

I lay on the floor of your empty room
and stared at the ceiling of white,
screaming your name again and again
until my throat burned with fire
and my lips cracked and bled.

You did not answer.

I crawled like a baby,
teary-eyed and broken,
clinging to the past and wishing away today.
For a moment I prayed
for death to take me too.

But all it did was sneer.

One by one, I removed your clothes
from their white plastic hangers
and emptied out your dresser drawers.
Your scent, familiar and sweet,
lingered in the air for a moment.

And then it was gone.

I thought, for a moment, your face I glimpsed
but it was just the shadow of a cloud
moving across the wall.
I thought, for a moment, your voice I heard,
alive and sanguine like before,
but it was just the sage-scented breeze.

And nothing more.

FOREVER DANCING

Silently the angels weep
as I lie in dreamless sleep;
tears they shed upon the stones
bequeath no comfort to my bones.

Mournful wings bleak shadows cast,
veil my name claimed by the past.
Entombing as a six-foot hole,
eternal like my wintry soul.

Cry not for me,
weep not a breath.
I'm not alone;
I dance with Death.

FORGET ME NOT

Forget me not when murmurs the wind
and dead leaves in the graveyard dance,
when storm clouds gather high above,
remember me forever, my love.

When withering flowers hang low their heads
perfumed with death's aroma sweet
and cold rain blurs the window glass
there I shall be, my precious love.

When black-feathered birds sing sad their songs
and ghostly mist in meadows looms
and dew, like pearls, cling to the webs,
forget me not
forget me not.

FREAKS

Naked we stand
for all to see.
No more secrets to hide,
no more corners of the mind
to hide in.

Like clowns with radio-active
eyes, and bearded ballerinas
dancing, we are all freaks
in a lunatic circus
of the bizarre.

Walking high on wires
electrified, defying death
with arrogant self-confidence,
we live our lives behind
faces smiling, frowning
masks of polyurethane...
The crowd cries out for more.

Hurry! Hurry!
Step right on in;
the circus sideshow is about
to start!
Naked we stand
for all to see;
each one of us a freak
in a transparent jar.

FROM OUT OF THE ABYSS

In a dark and dreamless hour it came,
with claws and fangs,
from out of the abyss.
Hideous, disrupting the night
into black jigsaw puzzle pieces.
Exploding like a supernova;
a scream like no other.
It shook the walls.
It dripped with blood.
Appalling.
Horrific.
Deafening.

My heart went still.
My mind, disoriented, swirled like haze.
My muscles tensed. My fingers trembled.
And then, again, it shattered the night.
Murderous.
Consuming.
Conjuring a madness from deep within
the bowels of the earth.

Again and again it rang out.
Louder and louder!
Over and over!
Like a knife blade stabbing,
deeper and deeper!
Until the stained-glass windows imploded
and with pain my ears did throb.

And the castle walls cracked and crumbled away.

And then, all at once,
the screaming
stopped.

The silence returned. The throbbing ceased.
I realized the screams were mine...
And the cold night exhaled a sigh.

GRAY MANOR

A crumbling, moldering mansion am I,
high on a hilltop I silently stand.
Haunted by ghosts that are chained to the past,
bleak apparitions that weep in the night.

Secrets are hidden inside bricked-up walls
shielded by tapestries, frayed and decayed.
Chandeliers, cobwebbed, once brilliant and grand
fallen like angels on dusty floors, smashed.

Portraits in hallways with faces misplaced;
dead people's images, names forgotten.
Rooms cold and empty, void of a heartbeat.
Perilous stairwells that only lead down.

Doors are shut tightly, locked, never opened;
keys that once freed them, corroded by tears.
Stygian shadows protect my ruins.
No one may enter, and no one may leave.

Windows like tormented eyes that observe
the smiles of the people that pass outside,
Laughing, their voices echo in madness
cracking the panes into fragmented blurs.

A crumbling, moldering mansion am I,
weathered, decrepit, I silently stand.
Embedded with memories, painful smiles,
knowing the bulldozer's blade is coming.

GRAY SKIES

Gray skies dance in my lover's eyes
reflect my crippled soul.
Gray skies weep for our love's demise
but never can console.

Gray skies hide all my tears opaque
behind their crystal rain.
Gray skies are filled with shadows dark,
endless, unconstrained.

Gray skies flow through my pulsing veins
above my grief they laugh.
Thunder and lightning stir my brain;
each one an epitaph.

Gray skies form into marble thoughts
and dreams and memories,
but soon they commence to crumble down
like swords of Damocles.

THE GREEN-EYED MONSTER

"Goddamn it, Wendell! Must you always slurp your soup like that?" Beverly asked her bespectacled husband. Her words reverberated with vexation, and the grating quality of her voice was comparable to the noise produced by fingernails scraping against a chalkboard. "You have absolutely no idea how revolting the sounds that you make when you eat are to me. Or maybe you do it deliberately just to get under my skin. That's it, isn't it?"

"I'm sorry, dear," Wendell replied. "I would never dream of getting under your skin. In fact, Beverly, I can assure you in all sincerity that under your skin is not a place that I would care to venture." He returned to his soup slurping.

"You strive to make my life as miserable as possible," Beverly declared as she checked with her fingertips to ensure that her pink hair curlers were still securely in place. "It's like your mission in life," she continued. And you know what, Wendell? You succeed in doing it on a daily basis!"

"I'm sorry, dear," Wendell replied, meekly. He was a man of few words – especially when it came to his harpy of a wife. Over the years, he learned through experience that the less he said to her, the smaller were his chances of enkindling her easily aroused wrath. He removed his glasses that were fogged up by the steam of the hot soup and wiped the lenses clear with his paper dinner napkin.

"Oh don't give me that crap," snapped Beverly as she lit up a cigarette, her snarling lips staining half of the white filter tip with a tacky coating of lipstick in a shade of fire-alarm-red. "You and I both know that you aren't sorry about a damn thing."

Wendell put down his soupspoon and cleared his throat. "Well," he began, rather cautiously and without taking his eyes off his bowl of soup, "that isn't quite entirely true, dear. There are one or two things that I _am_ sorry about."

"Oh? And I suppose marrying me is one of them?" inquired Beverly, glaring at her husband from across the small kitchen table. Her gaze was like the stab of a sharp dagger, and if looks could kill, she would have acquired the status of widowhood decades ago. "Why don't you just come right out and say it?"

Wendell wiped a dribble of soup from his bottom lip with his napkin, and then exhaled a tired-sounding sigh.

Beverly took a deep drag on her cigarette and blew the smoke out in one big puff in Wendell's direction. She then smashed out the cigarette into the seashell-shaped ashtray on the table.

"Well, let me tell you something," she began. "If anyone in this kitchen should be sorry about that, it's me!" she shouted, and a tiny bit of spittle flew from her mouth and landed on the lenses of her husband's glasses. Pushing her chair away from the table, she grumbled, "I wasted the best years of my life on you with high expectations that you were going to make it as a world-renowned anthropologist. But your ludicrous treatises on the mating habits of Bigfoot got you laughed right out of the University. And to think, I could have married an architect!"

She sashayed over to the window overlooking the seemingly endless forest. Rays of afternoon sunlight filtered through the pine needles and danced upon the leaves of the locust trees, which were hinting of golden yellow as a reminder that autumn was on the horizon.

All at once the chirping of the birds outside died away and an eerie hush fell over the woods. Beverly thought she saw a dark hulking figure run through the forest, weaving in and out of the trees. And then it vanished from sight. She dismissed it as some kind of wild animal, perhaps a large bear.

"Every other month you drag me up to this spider-infested cabin in the middle of the godforsaken wilderness," Beverly complained, turning back to glare at her husband. "I'm almost positive that you do it just to drive me out of my mind with boredom. Well, here's a news flash, Wendell. Sitting around in this dump a million miles from civilization with only you for company isn't exactly my idea of a rip-roaring good time. Why can't we ever go on a real vacation like the Sinclairs? This past summer they spent three whole weeks on the French Riviera. And the Goldfarbs, they just got back from an African safari!"

Beverly's nostrils were suddenly assaulted by a strange and putrid stench that sent her stomach reeling with nausea.

"What on earth is that revolting smell?" she asked, waving her hand in front of her nose and contorting her face in disgust. "Oh my God! Is that coming from you, Wendell?"

"No, dear," Wendell answered. His lips cracked a slight smile as though he were privy to a private joke.

"Ugh!" Beverly groaned while wrinkling up her nose. "Whatever that rancid smell is, it's simply ghastly and it's making my stomach turn. Oh, I need to open the window to let some fresh air in!"

She unlatched the lock that secured the window and threw open the sash. However, her expectation of a breath of fresh air was not fulfilled, as the foul stench grew even stronger now and appeared to be emanating from outside of the cabin.

"Oh my God!" Beverly vociferated. "It smells like something died out there! I don't know why I always let you talk me into coming up here all the time. This place is appalling. Did you hear what I said, Wendell? It's truly appalling!"

Just as she was about to pull down the sash, a monstrous hair-covered face with large glowing eyes of green appeared outside the open window and curiously peered in at her. In immediate response, Beverly's eyes widened in terror and from her mouth blasted forth a loud, blood-curdling scream, which scared some of the birds out of the nearby trees, but unfazed her mild-mannered spouse.

"Wendell!" she cried out as she slowly backed away from the face at the window. "There's some kind of huge hideous animal outside the window staring at me! Do something about it!"

The creature began to emit loud grunting sounds, which triggered another scream from the terrified woman. Beverly's body shook with fear, causing one of her pink hair curlers to loosen and fly from her head.

"Wendell!" she cried. "Don't just sit there! Go get the rifle! Quickly! This thing... whatever it is... is getting ready to attack! Wendell! Did you hear me?"

"There's no need for you to panic, dear," Wendell stated with the utmost calmness attached to his voice. He proceeded to light up his pipe like he did after every meal and took a few puffs on it. The tobacco smoke tantalized his taste buds with its sweetness. "That 'thing' as you call it is just a female Sasquatch. You see, Beverly, as I've told you before, they do exist. She won't harm you. Unless, of course, you insist on making her feel threatened, which is a propensity that you've become quite masterful at over the years."

"Well," said Beverly in a huff, "if you aren't going to be a man and do anything about it, then I'll have to take care of things myself... just like in the bedroom!" She then rushed across the cabin and retrieved the loaded .22 caliber long rifle that was hanging on the wall over the mantel of the stone fireplace.

Wendell's calmness instantly evaporated into thin air and he jumped up from his seat, clearly agitated. "What on earth do you think you're doing?" he asked in an uncharacteristically bold voice. "Put that gun down, Beverly! Put it down right this instant!"

"Like hell I will!" Beverly yelled, returning to the window with the firearm in her hands. She then cocked the gun and aimed it at the Sasquatch, which continued to peer in. The creature stared into her eyes with a look of contempt and let out a deep, guttural growl.

"I forbid you to shoot her!" yelled Wendell. His normally meek-sounding voice was now tinged with outrage and rang with an unusual assertion that took his wife aback. "She's with child and due to give birth any day now!"

"Oh?" said Beverly, curiously. "And just how do you know so much about this… this… knocked-up monster and its baby?" She glared at her husband and waited impatiently for him to reply.

"Because I'm the father," Wendell replied emphatically.

"You're the what?" said Beverly in an exaggerated tone of disbelief. "This is no time to be cracking jokes, Wendell! You've never been any good at delivering a punch line. Have I ever told you that the only funny thing about your jokes is your inability to be funny?"

"It's no joke," said Wendell. "I'm afraid I'm quite serious. If you must know, I impregnated her last December. I've been closely monitoring the progress of her gestation, and when my documentation on the first successful interspecies mating between human and Sasquatch knocks the world on its ear, I'll finally be awarded the recognition due to me from that pretentious university!"

Several moments of silence passed and then Beverly began to cackle with uncontrollable laughter befitting a wart-nosed witch stirring a cauldron bubbling with hell-broth.

"Are you seriously expecting me to believe that you screwed a Bigfoot?" she asked in between her cackles.

Wendell nodded his head.

Beverly's laughter soon faded away as she came to realize that Wendell's confession of infidelity had been spoken with sincerity. Rage began to build up inside of her and then erupted like a volcano spewing molten lava. Seething, betrayed, and humiliated, she turned the gun on her unfaithful husband and the color in his cheeks went pale.

"You bastard!" she screamed, and then she squeezed the trigger.

The handle of the rifle kicked back and knocked another one of Beverly's pink curlers off her head as a loud shot rang out and a bullet exploded through Wendell's abdomen, leaving a gaping hole. It struck the knotty pine wall behind him and became lodged in the wood. Clutching his blood-gushing bullet wound with his hands, he collapsed onto the floor. A puddle of blood began to quickly spread around his twitching body.

A glowing feeling of satisfaction instantly washed away Beverly's pent-up rage as she observed the aftermath of the gunshot. And then the sobering realization of the seriousness of the situation began to sink in, filling her with alarm.

"Oh Jesus! Now look what you made me do," she complained. "I hope you know this is all your fault. You're nothing but a pig, Wendell."

The green-eyed creature suddenly let out an ear-piercing wailing noise that made Beverly's blood run cold as ice. With her rage renewed, she aimed the gun at the Sasquatch and fired, but the bullet missed its mark and hit the frame of the window instead. The creature took off running and despite its advanced state of pregnancy, it moved with great agility and speed. Beverly rushed back to the window, took aim and fired the gun once more, but again she missed.

"Damn it!" she growled as she watched the fleeing creature disappear into the shadows of the forest. Blowing her chance to kill the child-carrying cryptid that her unfaithful husband had bedded, enraged her for a few brief moments, and then her thoughts turned back to the matter at hand.

Beverly plopped back down in her chair in the kitchen and reached for her pack of cigarettes that sat on the table. Annoyed to discover there was only one cigarette remaining in the pack, she cursed her bad luck underneath her breath, lit up her last smoke, and then pondered what to do about her husband's dead body.

She suddenly remembered the shovel and pickaxe that were out in the shed behind the cabin. She decided she would go out into the woods and dig a grave as deep as she could. Once Wendell was buried, she would then burn the cabin to the ground and drive home. She would also fabricate a story that Wendell packed his bags and left her. It was a tale she felt sure nobody would have any trouble believing, as the couple's contempt for each other was well known within their small circle of friends.

Beverly located a spot in a small clearing off the path near a babbling brook that she felt would make an ideal gravesite. With the loaded rifle and a kerosene lantern by her side, she began the laborious task of digging. From a branch high up in a pine tree, a curious blue jay observed.

"God damn you, Wendell," she cursed through her clenched teeth in an irritated-sounding voice as she paused to catch her breath and to blot the beads of perspiration from her face with a handkerchief. "You always create work for me."

Beverly toiled away into the night and sighed with relief when she finally had the hole completely dug. She then made her way back to the cabin by the light of the kerosene lantern and was looking forward to a well-earned rest and a glass or two of blackberry brandy before dragging her husband's corpse through the woods, rolling it into the waiting grave, and filling it back in with dirt. As she neared the door, she heard several loud knocking noises coming from somewhere in the forest, which sounded like a rock being struck against a tree.

She hurried to get back inside the cabin, quickly shutting and locking the door behind her. She placed the rifle and kerosene lantern upon the table and set off to retrieve a bottle of brandy from the kitchen cupboard. A loud gasp escaped from between her lips when she discovered that Wendell's body was no longer on the floor where she had left him earlier. From the large pool of dried blood that marked the spot where his body had landed after sustaining his gunshot wound, a long trail of smeared blood led across the floorboards to the bedroom door. Beverly was aghast.

"Wouldn't that just be typical of Wendell," she mumbled to herself, "to be alive after I just spent over eight grueling hours digging a grave for that man?"

She followed the trail up to the bedroom door and called out, "Wendell? Are you in there? Are you still alive?"

No sound came from the other side of the door.

Beverly placed her hand upon the knob and turned it as a flutter of anticipation spread from the pit of her stomach to the tips of her fingers. She opened the door very slowly; unsure of what would be waiting for her inside the room. All at once, an all-too-familiar putrid stench assailed her sense of smell, and she gasped with horror and cringed at the nightmarish sight that unfolded before her eyes.

She initially thought that her eyes were deceiving her, but as she realized that what they were showing her was indeed real, fear slashed through her body like a hot blade and she felt herself trembling like the ground when fault lines release their built-up tension. She felt a scream rising up in her throat, but no sound would issue forth from her mouth.

There upon the blood-soaked mattress of the bed lay Wendell's body, unmoving and slightly bluish in color.

His eyes and mouth were gaping just as they had been when Beverly left the cabin to dig his grave. At his side was the pregnant Sasquatch, and gathered around the bed as if in silent vigil stood half a dozen more of the gigantic humanoid creatures. Their massive bodies were covered by glossy black hair and their heights ranged from seven to eight feet tall. They all turned their grotesque faces in Beverly's direction, bared their sharp yellowish teeth, and growled with such volume and ferocity that Beverly was sure she could feel the floor beneath her feet vibrating.

The scream that had been stuck in her throat now managed to find its way out of her mouth and she turned and ran towards the door leading outside. The growling Sasquatch creatures bolted after her, clawing at the air with their black and leathery paw-like hands.

Beverly's adrenalin was pumping like an oil well in Texas as she frantically fumbled with the latch. She managed to unlock it and flung open the door, fleeing from the cabin into the pitch-blackness of the forest. Without the kerosene lantern, she had to rely solely on the pale rays of the waning moon that shone down through the dense canopy of the treetops to light her way. She could hear the frightful sounds of the creatures growing louder as they gained on her, and she ran as fast as she could. Her feet stumbled over jagged rocks and gnarled roots. Tree branches that impeded her path, invisible within the dark cloak of night, clawed her face and arms.

Panic-stricken and with her vision obscured by night blindness, Beverly had no idea where she was or in what direction she was heading. All she knew was she had to keep running to avoid being captured by the growling creatures pursuing her.

As she ran through the forest like a frightened deer, she began to wonder what horrible things the Sasquatch would do to her if they caught her. Would they tear her apart and devour her flesh until all that remained were her skull and bones? Or would they gang rape her and impregnate her with some sort of hellish half-human monster? Would that be their retribution for Wendell having impregnated one of their own?

Beverly's pondering came to a quick end as the solid ground underneath her feet suddenly disappeared without warning. She felt herself plummeting, and within a matter of seconds she landed with a thud on the hard ground at the bottom of the deep hole she had dug for her husband's body, and several more pink curlers flew out of her sweat-drenched hair. Upon impact there came a loud snapping noise from her left shin, followed by excruciating pain. With her fingers she could feel the broken end of her tibia bone protruding through the skin. Blood ran like a river from the wound, dampening the ground under her leg. Beverly battled with herself to keep from crying out from the agony. She clenched her teeth tightly and contorted the muscles in her face. Tears were rolling down her cheeks.

Realizing that it would be impossible for her to outrun the Sasquatch with her leg in the sorry state it was now in, she figured the only thing she could do at that point was stay hidden in the hole and try to keep as quiet as possible so they wouldn't be able to locate her. She reassured herself that it would be sunrise in just a few hours and she would make an attempt then to pull herself out of the hole.

Just then, she heard the sound of twigs snapping nearby. It was soon followed by the dreaded putrid stench, which wafted ominously into the hole. Beverly held her breath and feared that the pounding of her heart would give her away. She then saw the faces of the Sasquatch peering down at her from the top of the hole. They grunted and wailed, and then, to Beverly's astonishment, they were gone. She exhaled a sigh of relief.

However, minutes later they returned with armloads of large rocks, which they began dropping into the hole. One hit Beverly's broken leg and she howled in pain. And then, using their large hands as shovels, the hairy creatures began filling in the hole with the mound of soil that Beverly had piled up next to it. The terrified woman screamed hysterically and struggled to climb out of the hole as it rapidly filled in with dirt and rocks.

A terrifying thought suddenly flashed through Beverly's mind. *Oh my God! These creatures are trying to bury me alive!*

Before she knew it, the backfill had completely covered her, and she gasped desperately for air, but was only able to fill her lungs with particles of dirt. Exerting all the strength that remained within her, she fought to claw her way out of the earthen tomb that held her captive. However, the heaviness of the dirt and rocks rendered her incapable of moving her extremities.

The green-eyed monster and her clan listened as the woman's scream, muffled by the earth, rose up faintly and then was no more. They grunted wildly and howled with satisfaction before disappearing into the darkness of the forest.

The dawn kissed the dew-drenched forest with its soft rays of golden light while spiders diligently spun their silken webs between the branches of shrubs. The waking birds sang their chirping songs and the meandering brook gurgled as water flowed over its slick and shiny stones. Chipmunks scurried across paths paved with last autumn's fallen leaves. Purple morning glories bloomed, butterflies fluttered, and bees buzzed. And not far from the mound of a fresh grave in the middle of a small clearing, there came the sound of a baby's first cry.

136

THE END

THE GRIMOIRE

Oh ancient book
with symbols arcane,
your mystical key unlocks
the past.

Revealing the mysteries
of the ages
with words on century-faded
pages, and incantations
in tongues of old.

With magic imbued
you hold dark secrets,
the wisdom, and the power
of the oracles and sages.

You conjure the tempests
that rage in my heart,
and summon forth demons
that prowl my every desire.

GROUND ZERO

Inside a jar of man-made life
a child with radiation eyes
that never saw the sun
  never saw the sun...

Reflections dance inside his brain;
a seed is planted free of pain.
They grew him strong without a heart;
machines can always get new parts.

And America did worship him;
to stay alive they had no choice
but to sing and dance for him
and sacrifice their children's toys
for one tear ends the world
one tear ends the world...

Assassins from the other side
killed the child without a soul.
His head glowed bright atomic light:
Four,
  Three,
    Two,
One,
    Ground Zero...

And now it's too late to turn back;
the earth is fading into black
and soon your mind will turn to rust
and all your dreams will turn to dust.

Gerri R. Gray

You'll fall so dead
the pins will fly out of your head.

HAIKUS OF HORROR

Rotting flesh and fangs
Hungering for human meat
Return from the dead.

Silently the blood
Flows into rivers of gore
Madness stalks the streets.

Cemetery mist
Dances ghostly in the night
Hands reach out from graves.

Cobwebs and shadows
Dusty trunks in attic locked
Gruesome riddles hide.

Pyramids of stone
Ancient altars to the sun
Sacrificial blood.

In the dead of night
Footsteps sound in empty rooms
Shadow people dance.

Necronomicon
Conjures things not of this world
Old Ones awaken.

The mark of the Beast
Manifests in loving eyes
Number 6-6-6.

Lifelike mannequins
Hideous secrets hidden
Underneath the wax.

> Black leather midnight
> Faceless figures reappear
> Night demons taunt me.

Kiss of the vampire
Bloodstained lips that call my name
Moist with death so sweet.

THE HAUNTED STARS

Lost in a realm of shadows,
I wander in search of
a flickering flame.
I look in your eyes but find darkness.
Your soul is a sky filled with haunted stars.

Trapped in a world of phantoms,
in circles that hold no
beginning or end.
I run through a night lit by neon
and wake in a dream of recurrent screams.

Chained to a heart of madness,
the haunted stars gather
and spell out your name.
I fall to my knees in exhaustion,
and bit by bit
I
slowly
disappear.

HERE I AM

Purple darkness beckons;
the harsh night calls my name.
Here I am, a shadow-child,
outside looking in.

The hunger in my cold heart,
the thirst that pales my lips
draws me like a dying moth
closer to your flame.

Your touch is warm and gentle,
you make me feel alive.
Here I am, the velvet ghost
of things the past has claimed.

Silent towers grimace
above our blood-stained joy,
Whilst hauntingly you gaze,
amazed, deep within my eyes.

No promise of tomorrow
will you find there, my sweet love,
For in my eyes the sun sets only;
never does it rise.

HIEROGLYPHIC DREAMS

Forgotten lovers and strangers
paint their images in my brain
with meaningless shapes,
with meaningless lines,
and words from poetry out of rhyme.

With secret symbols they gesture,
hieroglyphs that turn to strange
abstract blurred Picasso faces
for my perception to evade.

Disarranging my solitude,
my understanding now transformed
into confusion, fragments, thoughts...
and in the translation
their message is lost.

I AM SHE

I am She...
a blazing star of many colors,
a universal mind of many dreams.
I am the fertile earth,
the sacred garden that gives life
to the seed.

I burn like the golden sun
I shine like the silver moon
I rise and fall like ocean tide.

I am She who spills her blood
upon sacrificial altars
where magic and miracles
are performed.

I am the Creatrix
the cycle of life, unceasing,
the elements and the seasons,
forever changing and timeless.

I am She of ten thousand names.
I am She of a trillion faces.

I am the Spell-Caster,
the Dream-Weaver,
Storm-Bringer...

I am Goddess,
I am Woman,
I am She.

IN LAMPBLACK EVENING SOLITUDE

In lampblack evening solitude
I sit in the parlor, watching time
gradually slide by.
Each minute stretches into a
lifetime of failures and regrets.
Each hour transforms into eons.

I fill your heirloom cup with the tea
you always liked, even though your lips
will never taste it.
I converse with the image you left behind,
remembering the sound of your voice
like a chord trailing off
in the wind.

The clock ticks in rhythm
with the beats of my heart,
both growing old and feeling weary

In lampblack evening solitude
your memories creep
under my bedroom door
like winter's icy fingers.
They climb into my bed and
enter my sleeping head,
leaving me to toss and turn and
awaken, wrapped in a cold
sheet of sweat.

Your pillow, untouched, is a grim
reminder that the rain on the panes
is now my only companion.

IN MY GARDEN GRIM

In the cold dismal rain
I buried my tears
like seeds in a garden
of autumn's withered dreams.

Soon the brown leaves of death
did cover the ground
and rot with the sweetness
of decomposing grief.

Then the bleak falling snow
did blanket the earth;
my tears were forgotten
in winter's frozen grip.

On the first day of spring
they sprung from the earth
and bloomed like clusters
of mourning glories blue.

IN THE REALM OF FAERIE

In the realm of faerie
dreams enchanted lie.
Time is timeless in its spell
and one can never die.

In the realm of faerie
magic weaves the night.
In circles spun from spider silk
their potions will delight.

In the realm of faerie
fascination does abound,
but take care not to step upon
a faerie dell or mound.

You'll surely find their circle gay,
a charming citadel,
but one whole year shall be your day
when bound are you in spell.

IN THE VIOLET OBSCURITY

In the violet obscurity of a joyless twilight,
in graveyards I walk alone, echoless,
on carpets of spongy moss and creeping phlox,
past long-forgotten tombs and nameless crypts
that weep shadows for the death of sunbeams.
A cold wind arises as the orange horizon
bids a sad farewell.
Memories of you, and of us
tumble cruelly through my mind
like windswept leaves, helpless,
directionless.
Words, like daggers, pierce my heart;
their poisoned tips swim in my blood,
tainting the remnants of my hopes.

In the violet obscurity of a joyless twilight,
I hunt with desperation for resolve,
but reflections of things that once were
are all that I find.
I look to stone sentinels for comfort
but all they can offer is indifference.
And then, bursting up through the dirt,
a clawing hand! Putrid and horrid.
A hand of decomposition…
my hand.

I scream and run,
trip and fall like the darkness.
My bones shatter. My mind careens.
Silent laughter fills the air
as I feel my insignificance growing
malignant like a cancer.

I reach out for your hand to help me up
but a frosty wind is all I feel
biting at my flesh.
I yearn for yesterday
but, like my salvation,
it is buried too deep to exhume.
The sky, now indigo and starry
becomes a shroud for my corpse.
The netherworld of your eyes
as I remember them
becomes my open grave.

Gerri R. Gray

ISIS LIVES AGAIN

Desert winds howl, sandstorms bite,
the claws of Bast rip apart the night,
merciless and sharp as razors;
Tremble the priests and old stargazers.

The Pharaoh moon, like a falcon rises,
majestic is her face of gold.
Thunder cries, earthquakes rumble,
calling forth the gods of old.

And now the rivers' water and mud
thicken and flow red with blood.
Bells ring in the temples,
the pyramids tremble
for Isis lives again!

Friend to slaves and rulers alike,
protectress of the dead,
her magic fills a corpse with life
and fills her foes with dread.

Her breath is the wind
that caresses the Sphinx.
Her eyes are the shadows
that dance on azure seas.
A fiery Phoenix from the ashes reborn,
she rules from the throne of eternity.

LADY OF THE STORMY SKIES

She is the lady of gray stormy skies,
she is the watcher with white marble eyes.

> Standing in silence, a ghost from the past,
> haunting the living, dark spells does she cast.

Goddess of graveyards and shadows that creep,
bathed in the teardrops of widows that weep.

> Standing forever 'neath gray stormy skies,
> sculpted from sorrow, but never she cries.

LAPSUS LINGUAE (A Slip of the Tongue)

Some men speak with dragon breath
and acrimonious tongues of fire.
Some men talk in alien tongues,
smooth tongues, twisted tongues,
tenacious French kisses,
tongue to tongue.

Some tongues are square,
some tongues are cool;
rhyming and jiving,
fitting in perfect
tongue and groove.

With canting forked tongue
some men speak.
Others tell it like it is
with tongue in cheek.

Some tongues talk hip,
never at a loss for words.
Strung up and hung up,
stoned on the absurd.

Some cats talk old,
some cats talk young,
but always tongue-tied and baffled
when the cat's got their tongue.

Gerri R. Gray

LET ME SLEEP

Let my colors fade to gray,
let my spirit drift away;
no reason have your dark eyes to weep.
Let me sleep,
oh let me sleep.

I've tired of tasting bittersweet tears;
in salty seas I've drowned for years.
But place on my crypt a wreath of black
and never look back,
you mustn't look back.

Let your grief fade like the setting sun
in dying hues of orange and red;
my long-awaited joy shall be
found in the grave that cleanses my dread.

Do not disturb my dreamless keep
as I sleep, so deeply sleep
alone and where the stone angels weep
free from this web I've spun.

Let my colors fade to gray,
let my spirit drift away
like petals on a moon-kissed stream;
my journey's done and just begun.

LONELY WEDNESDAY

Lonely Wednesday
walking around...
outer space inside my head.
Looking at strangers
Ash Wednesday faces,
death masks bleeding in the rain.

Wednesday afternoon of black,
my storm cloud tapestries
are painted on the sky.
Haunted and hunted,
silent and still,
like avant-garde
self-portraits.

Lonely Wednesday child of woe
watches funerals from my window.
Shadow dreaming
in darkness and silence,
counting the raindrops
as they fall.

LOVE CAN MAKE YOU CRY

Love can make you cry,
love can make you fly so high
on wings of fire in the sky;
and that you cannot deny.

I was born to love you
like a thousand times before,
and I will cry
a thousand tears for you
'til I can cry no more.

Love shines like gold rings
but it doesn't mean anything,
it's just another song to sing.

Open up your eyes and see
it's just another fantasy;
you can't buy a dream
but reality is free
and it can make you cry.

Love will make you cry
the way you made me cry.
If you turn back the
hands of time,
never let your mind unwind
for tears are all you will find.

THE MADDENING CRY

England - 1647

Matthew opened his eyes and stared into the thick darkness that surrounded him. His slumber had not been peaceful. In despite of being the finest witch-finder and executioner in all of England, he was a man who always slept quite soundly. However, this night was different for him. A horrific nightmare had tormented his mind with a scene that struck terror within his heart and bathed his body in a cold sweat.

In a frightful and most peculiar dream, he found himself lying still upon a bed with his arms crossed over his chest in the manner of a corpse. Six women draped in black surrounded him. Veils of black lace covered their faces, and their cries and loud disconcerting wails sliced through the blackness of the night like banshees presaging a death. He then heard the sound of footsteps, and two burly men approached the bed.

Without the utterance of any words, they took hold of his body, lifted it up from the straw mattress, and then carried it to a waiting coffin. Filled with terror, he attempted to free himself from their grips, but soon found that the power to move his arms and legs was foregone. He made an effort to open his mouth and cry out; however, his lips would not part for him despite his best efforts. His entire body was frozen and rigid in a paralytic state from which he was unable to snap out of. The sight and sound of the coffin lid closing above him filled his eyes and ears, and then, in the ensuing darkness, he heard shovelfuls of earth raining down upon the top of the lid, one after another after another, until a deathly silence overtook the noise and the nightmare came to an abrupt, and merciful, end.

Matthew inhaled deeply and then sighed with relief. It was just a bad dream; a mere figment of his imagination. The thought soon crossed his mind that his nightmare could very well have been the doings of some vengeful witch versed in the evil ways of poppet magic or some other diabolatry. He then let out a hearty laugh, confident that he would sooner or later discover the true identity of this creature and, with the purification of a blazing fire, command her corrupted devil-fornicating soul to an eternal damnation in the pit of hell.

He believed himself to be a pious man, despite the sadistic pleasure he derived from the brutal acts of torture that he inflicted upon the naked bodies of accused witches and warlocks in order to obtain their confessions. With each scream and with each cry of agonizing pain his heart would pump wildly in excitement. And even greater would be his arousal, bringing a delicious tingling to his loins, whenever his cruel, but necessary, duties as a servant of God to eradicate the scourge of witches from the land led him to pretty-faced young sorceresses possessing succulent bosoms and buttocks. Often he would have his way with them before his tortures disfigured their attributes and rendered them repulsive to the sight, despite his vows of fidelity that were spoken when he took Elspeth, the daughter of the local blacksmith, as his wife.

It was during Matthew's third year of marriage to Elspeth when a rumor that she used charms to bewitch a neighbor's cow began to circulate throughout the small village in which they resided. She was arrested and made to stand trial, shackled and bearing the bruises, welts, and lacerations inflicted upon her by her very own husband in his determination to force a confession from her. In spite of her rounds of torture, which included whippings, the crushing of her thumbs and big toes with a thumbscrew, and the flesh of her breasts being seared with a red-hot iron poker, Elspeth refused to confess to being a follower of the Old Religion. Her refusal to admit that she was in league with the devil infuriated Matthew and no matter how she wept and pleaded for her life, he took no pity upon her.

Not a single tear did Matthew shed on that dismal day in October when he stood and calmly watched as his wife was dragged, screaming, to a large wooden stake that had been erected in the heart of the village. After she had been securely tied to it with heavy ropes, Matthew set ablaze the straw and branches and logs that had been piled around the base of the stake. Elspeth's screams, along with the wild cheering of the bloodthirsty mob that had gathered to watch, could be heard throughout the countryside as the hungry flames of the bonfire engulfed her twitching body and her flesh sizzled and burned, filling the air with a putrid-smelling black smoke.

"Blasphemous heathen witch," Matthew said out loud to himself as the charred remains of his wife crumbled and fell into the glowing embers. "May God have mercy upon her wicked soul."

That was long ago and he had given little thought to it throughout the years that followed. Until tonight when he suddenly recalled that the face one of the veiled mourners in his nightmare bore a striking resemblance to Elspeth's. For some reason unknown to him, he found that to be rather disturbing. He tried to return to sleep but was overcome by a feeling of unease. He decided to get out of bed and read his Bible. His favorite passage was in Exodus and said, "Thou shalt not suffer a witch to live." Those were words by which he lived and earned his daily bread.

The witch-finder made a move to sit up, but immediately discovered that he was unable to raise his torso more than a few inches before being blocked by some strange obstruction that hovered above in the pitch-blackness of his room. Puzzled by the queerness of this thing, he then attempted to turn himself but found there to be what felt like walls close to his sides. He banged upon them a number of times with his fists in a fruitless effort to break through their restraint.

The walls and roof that surrounded him and afforded him little movement were solid and felt to Matthew to be a rough-hewn wood of some type. They gave off dull thuds in response to his blows but were steadfast in their refusal to budge. The air was now growing uncomfortably warm and steamy.

"What ungodly manner of witchery have I fallen under?" Matthew shouted from within his solid cocoon of darkness. "In the name of the Lord, I command that this cursed spell be at once broken!"

A harrowing minute, which felt like an eternity, passed. Matthew again attempted to sit up, confident in the power of his command, but found that the mysterious blockade that surrounded his body was still in place, unchanged. He then began to wonder if perhaps he was still asleep, and this strange predicament was nothing more than part of his foul nightmare. The thought brought some comfort to him and he lay still and silently prayed to wake up. And then came a faint voice from somewhere above. It was ghostly in its tones yet possessed a strange familiarity about it. It whispered his name, again and again, until Matthew's recognition of it made him shudder. It was the voice of Elspeth.

"Witch!" cried Matthew, angrily. "Do you deny that this sorcery is your doing? Why do you not leave me in peace, foul spirit?"

Elspeth growled, "I shall never leave you in peace, dearly departed husband of mine. I shall remain by your side in hell for all of eternity! That I promise you!"

"Dearly departed? But I am not yet dead!" Matthew cried. "I am very much alive. My heart within my chest continues to beat, albeit in somewhat of a flurry at present." His voice suddenly took on an audacious tone. "I am a servant unto the Lord, and Heaven has reserved a place for my soul."

"Yes, Matthew," said Elspeth. "Indeed, you are not yet one of the dead as I am; that much is true. But your time approaches with haste. As for the soul of which you speaketh, you do not possess one. And the only place reserved for you is in hell!" Her laughter once again arose like a tempest, filling Matthew with a sense of dread.

"Hold your tongue, filthy witch!" Matthew cried out. "You are but a fabricator of untruths. Why do you persist in tormenting me in this manner? Are the fires of hell not hot enough to keep you from bewitching my mind with a nightmare of my own burial?"

"Nightmare?" Elspeth chuckled, sounding rather amused. "No nightmare has plagued your sleep, my husband... my murderer. The mourners your eyes saw were quite real. The undertakers who attended to your lifeless body were quite real. Your burial, as the passage of time will soon convince you, was no figment of the imagination."

Matthew's heart began to beat wildly, and he thought at any moment it might explode out of his chest. "But how can that be possible?" he cried out, now realizing that the wood surrounding him actually was a coffin. "How can I continue to breathe as a living man, yet be buried in the cold and dark of the earth as the dead?"

"Don't you know, Matthew?" asked Elspeth in a mocking manner. "When you condemned me as a witch and took pleasure in watching me burn alive, you forgot to take care to remember that I was the only other person who knew the dreadful secret of your cataleptic curse. I'm afraid you've been mistaken for the dead and buried alive, and no one is wise to that fact, save for you and me. It's just our little secret, my love." Elspeth roared with vengeful laughter.

Matthew's maddening cry rang out and echoed inside his ears, nearly deafening him. He furiously pounded his fists on the unyielding coffin lid and frantically tried to claw his way out of the wooden funerary box until his fingers were broken and bloodied. Sweat poured out of his forehead and ran down his face, stinging his eyes and bringing a salty taste to his lips. His chest heaved as he desperately gasped for air.

Six feet above, the sound of Elspeth's laughter echoed through the mist-filled graveyard as her ghost tossed a bouquet of wilted flowers on top of her husband's fresh grave, which was marked only by a small wooden cross that stood slightly bent. With a smile on her vaporous face, she turned and slowly walked away as lifeless brown leaves danced in the icy wind. She paused for a moment to take one final look at Matthew's gravesite.

"I'll see you in hell!" she hissed before vanishing into the ethers.

THE END

MADNESS IN THE MANOR

When shadowy moonlight does veil the moors
with glimmers of silver and mist obscures,
the whispers of ghosts doomed to find no rest
lament in the wind in a tone distressed.

High on a hilltop, a manor of stone,
its bleak silhouette stands dark and alone.
Faded its glory, stagnant its spirit,
fearing its fables, no one goes near it.

Inside, the mourners are gathered in black,
each with their eyes on my solid gold plaque.
Like vultures they pick through my dreams to claim;
but none remember my face or my name.

Laughing hyenas, they squeal and dispute,
clawing each other to grab at the loot.
My casket they use to divide the spoils;
I cannot awake though my heart recoils.

With Grandmother's plates, they dine on my soul
until the first rays of morning unroll.
Hollow condolences deafen my ears;
the mourners depart with their souvenirs.

MAGNUM OPUS IN DECAY

Shadow-shrouded wilted flowers,
weathered wreaths on graves forlorn,
cobwebbed rooms in darkened towers
shun the misty rays of morn.

Thorny daggers moist with crimson,
candles bleak on altars dark,
dusty books, forgotten poems,
Puncture wounds without a mark.

Distant echoes, fragmentations,
mystic skies of topaz blue,
everlasting lamentations
haunt my dreamscape, now askew.

Tattered pages, aged and crumbling,
rhyming words that fade away,
bound with disillusionment,
my magnum opus in decay.

MALEVOLENT MOONRISE

I take his hand and gaze into
the feral redness of his eyes
as a malevolent moonrise
fills the forbidding sky.
I dance in the shadow-filled void
where once his soul reclined.

I close my eyes and darkness veils
but fails to extinguish my cravings
for his icy touch that brings
a sweet brutality, or calm
his cravings for the delicacy
of my trembling heart.

His fingers, like talons,
caress my naked breasts,
leaving pink scratch marks
on my creamy flesh.
His passion rises and his claws
cut deeper
until droplets of red appear.
With his tongue
he wipes them away.

With anticipation
my insides tingle.
With carnality I quiver
and moan.

His teeth, like fangs
sharp and glistening and filled

170

with animal hunger,
brush against my locks
of windswept hair.
They settle on the softness
of my willing throat
and then plunge
inside me.

A burning sting invades my flesh,
the pain lasts but a moment,
soon replaced by pleasures odd
as my warm nectar gushes
sweet and red
at the urging of his loving bite.

At that moment
I surrender, unable,
or perhaps unwilling,
to flee.

My ambivalence dissolves
in an acid bath of irrelevance.

As he partakes my blood
and draws his sustenance,
he sucks out my essence
and his soulless heart
rejoices in renewal.

The malevolent moonrise
watches from above,
offering no solace,
only evil murmurs.

MARCY'S DIARY

Dust particles danced like ghost-orbs in the shaft of late afternoon light that crept through the tiny window in the gable. The long-dead corpse of a housefly, drained of its juices, dangled from the time-ravaged remains of a spider's web that clung from the top corner of the frame near a semi-circular crack in the pane. A creak cried out from a dusty floorboard and then the rusty metal hinges of a cobweb-enshrined trunk groaned as the lid lifted up, releasing a pungent perfume of mustiness, and revealing its hidden treasures that had, for years, reposed in a shroud of darkness.

"Oh my god!" cried Janice Lemort with excitement. Her hazel-green eyes, which were ghoulishly made-up with thick, black eyeliner and dark purple eyeshadow, grew wide with astonishment. "There's an old diary inside this trunk! I bet it's *her* diary!"

Janice's younger sister, Marlayna, peered into the trunk with equal parts curiosity and trepidation. She then let out a bit of a gasp. "Do you really think it's Marcy's diary?" she questioned with a slight tremble in her voice. "The girl who used to live in this house?"

"Yes," Janice replied with glee. Some of her long, raven-black hair with startling streaks of bright red fell in front of her blanched face as she bent down to retrieve the diary. She brushed the strands away with her hand as she returned her torso to an upright position, taking care not to accidentally hook one of her fingertips on the stainless-steel ring that dangled from her pierced septum. "Marcy, the psychopathic girl who hacked her entire family to pieces with an axe while they slept, and then hanged herself from a beam right here in this very attic. It's amazing that this diary's been hidden away up here all these years!"

"Oh Janice, I wish you'd put that book back in the trunk and lock it," Marlayna pleaded. Her voice sounded distressed. "I don't like it one bit. It's giving off such an evil energy and really making my skin crawl."

Janice slowly ran her fingertips across the faux-leather cover of the diary, which was almost as black as the nail polish that darkened her long fingernails.

"Most of the people in this town keep pretty tight-lipped about the axe murders, even though they happened over twenty years ago," she said. "But there's this one girl in my math class, her name is Carla Bennett, and she told me the gory truth about what occurred in this house. Her uncle was one of the detectives on this case. He told her that all the walls and ceilings were completely red with splattered blood, and there were bits and pieces of human body parts lying all over the place! Chopped-off hands and feet... eyeballs... intestines..."

"Oh, shit!" exclaimed Marlayna, wrinkling up her face in repulsion. "That's totally disgusting! I think I'm going to throw up." She paused for a few moments. "Do you suppose our parents know what happened here?"

"Most likely," replied Janice as she opened the diary and began browsing through its yellowed pages. "I mean, I'm pretty sure it's a law that people have to disclose that kind of stuff when they sell you a house in this state. 'Stigmatized properties' I believe they're called. It's no wonder our parents got this place for so cheap."

"Well, I wish they had bought a different house in a different town," lamented Marlayna as a faint look of disquiet flickered in her eyes. "Cheap or not, I don't like this place at all. Something about it doesn't feel right. Do you know what I mean? Sometimes, at night when I'm alone in my room, I feel like something's watching me."

"Oh, stop being such a paranoid little mouse," Janice scolded her sister. "I think it's pretty awesome if you ask me. I mean, seriously, not every girl can honestly boast that she lives in a bonafide crime scene. Plus, the rumor going around school is that our house is haunted. And not haunted by just any old run-of-the-mill ghost, but by the evil spirit of the deranged axe murderess herself! I found that out from Carla Bennett too. What do you think of that?"

"I think you and your Goth friends are a weird bunch," Marlayna blurted out, shaking her head from side to side. "I'm going back downstairs. I've had enough of this attic and all this talk about Marcy."

Janice snickered, "You candy-ass!" She then made a monster face at her sister and added, in a put-on creepy voice, "You're just afraid that Marcy's ghost is lurking in the shadows."

"No, I'm not!" snapped Marlayna with a tone of indignation in her voice. "It's too hot and stuffy up here, that's all. And besides, I don't even believe in ghosts."

"You do so," Janice calmly contradicted, her eyes not looking up from the pages of the journal. "Hey! Check this out, Marlayna! The last entry in Marcy's diary is dated August 2nd, 1997 and says: 'I must bid you farewell, dear diary, as this will be my final entry. You've been my only friend and confidante for the past seven months, and I will miss you more than these mere words could ever express. I feel like I have finally woken up from a long dream that had my mind trapped like a helpless insect in the web of a huge spider. Tonight was the night I've waited sixteen years for. The deed is done and I'm free at last. There's no turning back from it now. The innocent lambs have been slaughtered, and all the King's horses and all the King's men can never put them back together again. Their deaths are my rebirth, and soon, dear diary, my soul will be gloriously united with the demon of shadows in the flames of the unholy for all of eternity. *Ave Satanas*.'"

Janice suddenly generated a wild-eyed look. "Oh my god, Marlayna!" she exclaimed, excitedly. "There's even a bloody smudge mark at the bottom of the page! Take a look!"

A sudden gust of wind conjured forth a ghostly wail as it rattled the windowpanes like some frightful invisible entity desperate to find its way inside the attic. The shadows in the corners seemed to grow a bit darker, and an icy tingle slithered along Marlayna's spine.

"I'm out of here," she abruptly declared, as Janice cracked an amused smile. Goosebumps were beginning to spring up on the young girl's forearms and it felt as though some of the honey-blonde hairs at the back of her neck were standing on end.

Wasting no time, Marlayna dashed to the door, and then scurried down the creaky wooden stairs that lead from the dark and musty confines of the attic to the sunlit second floor. Within a matter of seconds, she was gone from sight.

Unable to contain her laughter any longer, Janice's black-painted lips parted slightly and she let out an impish giggle. She placed the diary back into the trunk and shut the lid.

"Good night, dear diary," she whispered with a grin.

That night, Marlayna restlessly tossed and turned in her bed. She opened her eyes and glanced over at the eerie green glow of the digital clock that sat upon her nightstand, along with a dancing ballerina music box. Three o'clock. She shut her eyes once more and began counting backwards from one thousand in her head. She had read somewhere that it was an effective technique for inducing sleep.

She had reached 969 when a sharp, shrill cry came from Janice's bedroom, which was directly across the hall from hers. Without hesitation, Marlayna sprung up out of her bed and rushed to her sister's room to check on her.

"Janice! Are you all right?" Marlayna asked, switching on the light.

Janice was sitting up in her bed. Her face was clearly marked by a look of fright. "She was here! Oh, my God! She was in my bedroom!"

"Who was?" asked Marlayna with curiosity.

"Marcy," Janice replied. "She was standing right over there at the foot of my bed. She had an axe in one hand and she was covered in blood!"

"There's nobody in this room but you and me," Marlayna stated, looking around the bedroom. "And there's no blood on the floor or anywhere. You were just having a bad dream because of that diary up in the attic."

"No!" Janice protested. "It wasn't a dream, Marlayna. It was real. I don't care if you believe me or not, but Marcy was really here. And she even spoke to me."

"She spoke to you? What did she say?"

"Oh, my God," Janice whimpered, burying her face in her hands. "I don't even want to repeat the words. It's too horrible."

"Tell me, Janice!" Marlayna demanded. "What did she say to you?"

Janice went silent for a minute before replying to her sister. "She told me... that it's my destiny to kill everyone in this house, the same way she did. She said it has to be carried out because the demon wills it!"

The palms of Marlayna's hands started to perspire and her mouth went dry. "Janice," she began, her voice fraught with worry. "You're frightening me with that kind of talk. Marcy's dead. She committed suicide over twenty years ago. It was just a nightmare. It wasn't real."

There suddenly came the sound of something moving in the hallway, and then, to the horror of both sisters, the knob on the bedroom door began to turn. As the door slowly creaked open, Marlayna gasped and Janice shouted out, "Go away! Leave me alone!"

The door swung completely open and a feeling of relief instantly washed away Marlayna's mounting terror when she saw her parents enter the room.

"What's all this racket about?" asked Mr. Lemort. His voice vibrated with anger. "Do you girls realize that it's after three in the morning?"

"We heard screaming," Mrs. Lemort stated. "Is everything all right?"

"We're fine, Mom," Marlayna replied. "Janice just had a really bad nightmare, that's all. I came in to see if she was okay."

"I'm sorry," Janice apologized. "I didn't mean to wake everyone up."

"You look like you just saw a ghost," said a worried-looking Mrs. Lemort to Janice. She walked over to the bed and placed the back of her right hand upon her daughter's forehead to check for a fever. "Look at your face, honey. It's so pale. Are you sure you're all right?"

"Yes," Janice answered, sounding a bit annoyed. "I'm okay now. Really. I am. Everybody, just go back to bed."

As her parents exited the bedroom, her father ordered, "Get to sleep, you two. You both have school in the morning."

* * *

In her classes at school, that day, Marlayna found it difficult to concentrate on her studies. The teachers' words were but mere mumblings from some far-off galaxy that possessed neither meaning nor importance. All she could think about was Marcy and the axe murders. The dreaded image of the young murderess' diary haunted her brain, as did her sister's macabre dream that shattered the stillness of the early morning hours.

Could it have been more than just a nightmare? Marlayna pondered, while gazing out the window at nothing in particular. *Was it possible for Marcy's restless spirit to roam the earth, and did she have her sights set on possessing Janice? Could she actually manipulate Janice against her will to do her evil bidding?*

Marlayna's questions left her hungering for answers. The more she thought about Marcy and the diary, the stronger her uneasiness grew. She felt overcome by a feeling of helplessness and debated with herself whether or not she should inform her parents.

"Are we having a pleasant daydream, Miss Lemort?" thundered a sarcastic voice that startled her back to reality.

"I'm sorry, Mr. Krueger," Marlayna apologized, her cheeks turning red from embarrassment as giggles and whispering voices spread through the classroom.

"Not as sorry as you *will* be when report card time comes around," replied the teacher with an air of haughtiness. "If you fail this class, you'll never make the cut for college. I suggest you look sharp, young lady."

"Yes, Mr. Krueger," Marlayna answered meekly, while lowering her head as if in shame.

The teacher sneered at the girl and shook his head in disgust before making his way back to the front of the classroom and resuming his lecture. Every so often, he would shift his glance back to Marlayna and flash her a look of disapproval.

That afternoon, while walking home from school, Marlayna's ears detected an unfamiliar female voice softly calling out her name. She stopped and quickly turned around to look but found no one there. She was all by herself. A feeling of panic rose up inside of her and she began to run. It wasn't until she reached the long flagstone path leading to the front door of her house that she paused to catch her breath. She looked to make sure no one was behind her and then, feeling relieved, continued on her way.

However, no sooner had she resumed her walking, a strong gust of wind blew a yellowed and slightly crumpled page from a newspaper in front of her. Filled with curiosity, she crouched down and picked it up. It was dated the third of August 1997. As she un-crumpled the sheet of paper to read it, the bold words of an unnerving headline came into view: FAMILY OF 3 BRUTALLY AXED TO DEATH: KILLER COMMITS SUICIDE. Below it was a black and white photo of the same house that now stood before her.

Marlayna gasped. She suddenly felt light-headed and let go of the newspaper. As soon as it landed on the ground, another gust of wind picked it up and carried it off. Marlayna's eyes were then drawn to a figure moving behind one of the upstairs windows of the house. Gazing up, she could make out the face of a teenage girl. Pale. Expressionless. It stared down at her from Janice's bedroom with dark and cadaverous eyes.

Marlayna rushed into the house and found her mother in the kitchen preparing supper. She asked if Janice had a friend over and was told that her sister had not yet returned home from school. Marlayna then bolted up the stairs and, with adrenaline pumping in her veins, opened the door to Janice's bedroom and timidly stepped inside, panting. There was no sign of the girl she had seen at the window. And then the sound of a wire hanger falling on the floor emanated from the bedroom closet. Marlayna's heart was now racing with fear. She cautiously approached the closet, placed her hand upon the knob, and slowly turned it. She then yanked the door open and looked inside, only to find her sister's mostly black clothes hanging from a wooden rod. As she shut the door, she happened to look down. The sight of a wire hanger on the floor of the closet sent a shiver running down her spine.

During supper, Mrs. Lemort complained more than once that Marlayna had barely touched her food. She also made it no secret that she found her daughter's strange behavior to be rather worrisome. Janice, on the other hand, was oddly ravenous.

* * *

It was shortly after midnight when Marlayna awoke with a start. She popped open her eyes and gasped in horror at the sight of a raised axe blade illuminated by the light of the full moon that poured in from her bedroom window. For a moment, she thought she was dreaming, but soon realized that she was awake. She opened her mouth to scream.

"Shhh," Janice whispered. "Don't scream. It's only me."

Marlayna quickly sat up. "What are you doing in my room?" she asked. "And where did you get that axe?"

"It was hidden under one of the floorboards up in the attic," Janice answered. Her voice was oddly monotonal and devoid of any emotion. "Marcy came to me again tonight and lead me to it. She told me it was the same axe that she used to chop up her parents and younger brother with. If you look closely at the blade, you can see traces of dried blood on it."

An icy chill of fear gripped Marlayna, causing her to shiver. "If this is some kind of practical joke," she contended, "it really isn't very funny."

"I wish it were a joke," Janice stated, her eyes fixed upon her sister's, glazed and unblinking like the lifeless eyes of a cadaver. "But I'm afraid this is totally serious. Marcy explained it all to me, and now I know what I'm required to do. Don't you understand? I have no choice but to do it… for Marcy… and the demon of shadows."

"Janice! Cut it out!" cried Marlayna. "I can't tell if you're playing with my mind or if you've gone stark, raving mad. All I know is that you're really terrifying me right now! Put that axe down, for God's sake!"

"I'm sorry, Marlayna. It's too late for God."

Janice turned and ran from the bedroom, disappearing into the darkness that infused the hallway. A deathly silence fell over the house and lasted for a dozen seconds that seemed like an agonizing eternity. And then the screaming began. It was blood-curdling and so loud that it nearly drowned out the sound of the axe blade plunging into meat, again and again. The blows were relentless and filled with an uncontrollable rage. The sound of a lamp crashing to the floor commingled with the screams and cries for help, followed by a fit of maniacal laughter that dripped with evil like foam from the mouth of a rabid beast.

Marlayna immediately threw the covers aside and jumped out of bed, her heart pounding with rampant fear. Barefooted, she ran down the hallway in her babydoll nightgown of pink chiffon, screaming out, "Mother! Daddy!" As she drew closer to the master bedroom where her mother and father slept, the screams and horrible chopping sounds grew louder. And as she opened the door, her nostrils were assailed by the sickening, metallic smell of blood, and her eyes were filled with the horrendous sight of her crazed, blood-splattered sister delivering one blow after the other to her parents with the bloodied axe.

Her parents' king-size bedspread of white tufted chenille was soaked with so much blood that it appeared to be completely red. Splatters of gore clung to the light blue damask wallpaper and the ceiling like hideous pinwheels, and stomach-turning chunks of chopped flesh, like pieces of rare steak, lay about the room, oozing their juices.

"Oh, my fucking God!" Marlayna cried out, her eyes wide with disbelief, and her mouth gaping with unbridled horror. "Janice, what have you done?" Her body began to shake violently, and tears welled up and then streamed down her cheeks as the gory sight of her parent's hacked-up remains burned into her eyes like a glimpse into Hell.

Janice's insane laughter suddenly ceased, and she slowly turned her head in Marlayna's direction and made eye contact. "There is no Janice anymore," she growled in a gravelly, demonic-sounding voice. "There's only Marcy." She then raised the blood-smeared axe blade and, with frothy slime dripping from her lips, snarled, "It's your turn to die, bitch!"

An ear-piercing scream ejected from Marlayna's mouth and the horrified girl ran for her life, with her murderous sister in close pursuit. Halfway down the stairs, Marlayna lost her footing and tumbled the remainder of the way down until her battered body came to rest in a twisted heap on the hard parquet floor of the foyer. She could hear her sister's footsteps drawing closer and knew if she didn't act quickly she would be the next to die.

Ignoring the pain inflicted by the fall, Marlayna picked herself up from the floor and, at lightning speed, fled from her house of bloody horror into the crisp black night. She darted across the street to the old Queen Anne-style house where her teacher, Mr. Krueger, and his wife resided, and banged furiously upon their front door with her fists, all the while screaming, "Help me! Mr. Krueger! Help me!"

Moments later, the front porch light came on and Marlayna heard the sound of locks being unlocked. The door opened a crack and Mr. Krueger cautiously peered out, looking a bit groggy from just having been woken from his sleep.

"Marlayna?" he asked, sounding startled, as he was unaccustomed to finding one of his students at his front door in the middle of the night. "It's half past midnight. What on earth are you doing here at this ungodly hour?"

Marlayna's eyes were filled with tears and her body trembled uncontrollably. "Please!" she begged, her voice filled with desperation. "Let me in before she gets me too!"

"Before *who* gets you?" Mr. Krueger inquired, poking his head out the door and looking around. "There's nobody out there. You need to calm down, young lady. Have you been taking drugs or something?"

"No! You must believe me, Mr. Krueger!" Marlayna pleaded. "My parents… they're both dead! She killed them! She used the axe like Marcy! Oh, God! She's going to kill me too! It's all happening like in the diary!"

The baffled teacher opened the door wider and, with his hand, motioned for the terrified girl to come inside. He watched as she rushed into the house, and then he promptly shut the door and re-locked it.

"Who's at the door, Marshall?" a sleepy-eyed Mrs. Krueger called down from the top of the stairs. She craned her neck to get a look. "What's all the commotion down there?"

Mr. Krueger shouted up to his wife, "It's Marlayna Lemort from across the street. I'm not exactly sure of what's going on. The girl's hysterical. She said something about her parents being murdered. You'd better phone the police, Lorraine!"

"Oh, dear!" gasped Mrs. Krueger, and she scurried back to the master bedroom to make the call.

At that moment, the sharp and heavy blade of the axe split the wood of the Krueger's front door and Marlayna let out a terror-filled scream. She watched as her sister chopped her way through the door and then turned the axe on Mr. Krueger. The first blow struck his chest with a thud and blood spurted into the air like a geyser of bright red. A second blow sliced across his abdomen and his intestines spilled out onto the floor. The axe then hacked off his head and limbs and transformed the front parlor into a grisly scene of blood-soaked carnage and nightmarish gore.

In an effort to escape from the murderous rampage, Marlayna inadvertently stepped on one of Mr. Krueger's dislodged eyeballs and lost her balance. She fell forward and her forehead banged against the shelf of an antique whatnot that displayed Mrs. Krueger's extensive collection of vintage ceramic cats from around the world. Upon impact, she saw "stars" and then promptly blacked out.

* * *

The glaring light from an overhead incandescent bulb assaulted Marlayna's eyes as she slowly raised her eyelids. Her mind reeled with confusion upon finding herself sitting at a wooden table in the center of a tiny room. Her wrists were restrained by a pair of stainless steel handcuffs, and in front of her, on top of the table, sat a tape recorder. Sitting directly across from her was a strange man, who had a five-o'-clock shadow and appeared to be in his mid-to-late fifties. Draped over one side of his wrinkled pinstripe dress shirt was a brown leather shoulder holster, which contained a gun.

"Where am I?" asked Marlayna, looking around at her unfamiliar surroundings. "Why am I in handcuffs? Who are you?"

"I'm the detective and I ask the questions here," replied the man. His voice was harsh and carried a trace of a Boston accent. "Perhaps, now that you've had your little nap, you'd care to explain to me your motive for doing it. What possessed you to murder all those people?"

"What are you talking about?" Marlayna cried. "I didn't murder anybody! My sister, Janice, is the one who killed them! She's possessed!"

"Possessed?" asked the detective as he stared intently into the eyes of the agitated girl. "As in possessed by the Devil or a demon?"

"She was possessed by the spirit of a girl named Marcy," Marlayna explained, aware that her story probably sounded incredible to her interrogator, but hopeful, nevertheless, that he would believe her.

"Marcy," the detective echoed flatly. The tone of his voice was a clear indication to Marlayna that he was incredulous. He continued to stare at her without blinking.

"Over twenty years ago, Marcy and her family lived in the same house that my family and I recently moved into," Marlayna explained. "She went berserk one night and killed her entire family there with an axe. Janice discovered Marcy's diary in an old trunk up in the attic and it talks all about the murders and why she did it."

"Is this the diary you're referring to?" the detective inquired, tossing a small book with a black cover onto the table. He watched as the girl took it in her hands and then, after a moment, flung it back onto the table as though it were on fire and scorched her fingers.

"Yes," Marlayna answered, sobbing. "That's Marcy's diary. It's giving off an evil energy that's even stronger now than it was before. Can't you feel it?"

"Miss Lemort," began the detective, sounding annoyed, "I've lived in this town for almost sixty years, and I can assure you that, prior to the events of last night, no murders ever took place in the house that your family moved into. I've known all the families that have lived there and none of them had a daughter named Marcy. So how's about you stop with the bullshit and start telling me the truth?"

"But, I *am* telling you the truth!" Marlayna insisted, her voice growing excited. "A girl named Marcy *did* live there! And she *did* murder her family in that house! A girl in one of Janice's classes even told her about it, and her uncle was one of the detectives on the case. Plus, Marcy's confession, in her own handwriting, is inside that diary. There's the proof. Read it for yourself!"

"I *have* read it," replied the detective. "It contains only one entry, which our handwriting analysis expert confirmed was written by your sister, Janice." He picked up the diary, opened it, and read the entry out loud. "Dear Diary, I'm sorry to start you off on such a negative note, but I don't know who else to talk to about this. I know diaries are for writing down your thoughts and feelings, so here goes. I'm really worried about Marlayna. She's been acting weirder and weirder with each day that goes by, and seems to be totally obsessed with Marcy, even though I admitted to her that I made her up for a joke, along with the ridiculous axe murder story. She told me she's been having nightmares about Marcy and claimed that Marcy appeared in her room last night and demanded that she get an axe and slaughter everyone in the house while they sleep! I could hardly believe my ears when she told me that! Talk about creepy! I tried warning Mom and Dad that Marlayna was going off the deep end and maybe needs to get professional help. But, as usual, they never take anything I say very seriously. They just laughed it off, saying she has an overactive imagination and I shouldn't worry. But how can I not worry? She's my little sister and I feel extremely guilty for whatever it is that's happening to her mind. I wish now that I never invented the stupid story about Marcy. But you and I both know that wishes can't undo the damage that's been done."

"No!" shrieked Marlayna. "That's impossible! Those are all lies! Horrible lies! Janice read to me the entry that Marcy made in the diary. And then Marcy's ghost appeared in Janice's room that night and instructed *her* to kill everyone in the house with an axe, just like Marcy did over twenty years ago. Why don't you believe me? I'm telling you the truth! Where's Janice? She's the one who did it. You need to be questioning her, not me!"

For the first time since the interrogation session began, the detective cracked a slight grin. "Stop playing games with me, Miss Lemort. I think we both know that *that* isn't possible, now don't we?"

"Isn't possible?" Marlayna questioned, echoing the detective's words. Her confusion increased. "I'm afraid I don't understand. What are you talking about?"

"I'm talking about the fact that you brutally axed your sister to death, along with your parents and the Kruegers. We found your sister's decapitated head inside your bedroom closet when we searched the house. It was hanging from a coat hook by its nose ring."

With tears streaming down her cheeks, Marlayna let out a scream and jumped up from her chair. "That can't be! Janice was the one who committed the murders with Marcy's axe! I saw her do it! I'm not a murderess! I'm innocent!"

The detective stood up and pounded his right fist on the tabletop, angrily. "We have audio of Lorraine Krueger's 911 call to report that you broke into her house and were attacking her husband with an axe. We also found your fingerprints all over the murder weapon, Miss Lemort!" he shouted. "In fact, they were the *only* fingerprints on it! How do you explain all that?"

Marlayna let out a loud gasp of horror as the detective's words sent a chill down her spine and rattled her to the core. A cold sweat beaded up on her forehead and her breathing rapidly increased until she was hyperventilating. The room suddenly felt as though it was spinning and Marlayna grabbed onto the table with both of her hands in an effort to steady herself. Everything around her grew blurry, and then she fainted.

Hours later, while making her rounds, a tattooed female corrections officer was aghast to discover Marlayna Lemort's lifeless body hanging in her jail cell above a sickening puddle of bodily fluids. A clear plastic bag covered her head and wrapped tightly around her neck was an improvised noose fashioned from a bed-sheet. The dead girl's face was hideously bloated and bluish-gray in color, and her tongue, like a swollen purple serpent, protruded from her bloodstained, gaping mouth.

On the last page of Marcy's diary, which sat in a cardboard box in an evidence room at the police station next door, a new entry mysteriously appeared. It was scribbled in Marlayna's handwriting, and read:

> *"Dear Diary, You've been my trusted friend and confidante for some time; however, this will be my final entry. The nightmare that has spun its web around me has only one means of escape, and that is death. I have come to realize that,*

and I accept it wholeheartedly. I'm even looking forward to it. Before I go, I wish I could tell you why I felt compelled to murder all those people, but I honestly don't know. It's as much a mystery to me as to everyone else. I used to fear an imaginary monster under my bed when I was little, but the fear I feel now for the all-too-real monster that I've become is far greater. It must be stopped, or it will go on killing. Besides, how could I ever live with myself, knowing that I deliberately and brutally snuffed out the lives of the people I loved the most? Their screams continue to ring in my head. The look in their eyes just before I swung the axe blade at them continues to haunt me. Oh diary, I wish I could tell them all how sorry I am for what I did and how much I love them! But I know it's too late for that. Please forgive me for the horrors I've committed and for what I'm about to do. With a heavy heart, I bid you good-bye. Forever yours, Marcy"

THE END

MEMORY

MAUSOLEUM 13

The rusted hinges of the iron cemetery gate screamed out like a bird of prey in the night as Bradley Beauregard pushed the gate open. He made it wide enough for his girlfriend, Carly, and himself to slide through. From somewhere off in the distance, the eerie baying of a dog rose up and was carried away on the wind like an omen of something dreadful to come. The howling was like that of some diabolical beast, tormented and soulless, that was doomed for all eternity to roam the earth on death-cold nights such as this one.

"Hurry up, Carly," Bradley barked with impatience in his voice. "It's going to be midnight in less than twenty minutes. Must you always be so slow?"

"I'm coming," Carly answered as she squeezed through the crack of the gate and stepped inside the desolate cemetery. She pulled up her jacket collar to shield the bite of a chilling December gust. Apprehension tied a dark knot inside her stomach as snow flurries danced and swirled, ghost-like, in the air. The tiny frozen flakes landed upon her nose and cheeks, and immediately melted.

"I really don't like the idea of this, Bradley," Carly stated, nervously looking left to right. "I really think we ought to turn around and head back before someone catches us in here. I think it's against the law to wander around in a graveyard after sundown and I'm afraid of getting into trouble. My parents would kill me if I got busted – especially on Christmas Eve."

"Stop being such a coward," Bradley taunted. He rubbed the palms of his hands together in an effort to warm them. "I think what you're really afraid of is the legend."

"What?" Carly replied with a bit of a snicker. "The legend of mausoleum thirteen? Don't be ridiculous! I don't believe in that silly old wives' tale. That was made up a long time ago by a bunch of superstitious fools."

"You don't believe that if you knock thirteen times on the mausoleum's doors at midnight on Christmas Eve, the specter of death will answer?" Bradley inquired, cocking his head to one side.

"Of course not," Carly answered, rolling her eyes. "It's nothing but a load of bull. And I also don't believe the rest of the legend that he'll whisper in your ear the name of the next person destined to lie in the graveyard."

"You don't?" Bradley asked with a smirk on his face. "Well, I guess tonight you and I will find out if that legend is true or not. That is, unless you're scared, little girl." He then began making clucking sounds and moving his arms to imitate the flapping of wings.

"I'm not scared," Carly retorted. She then placed her hands upon her hips and a look of aggravation came over her face. "And must you always act so pathetically immature? I swear, Bradley, sometimes you act more like you're eight years old instead of eighteen."

The two teenagers trekked through the old cemetery past macabre statues of weeping angels, and white bronze obelisks. Row upon row of crooked and weathered gravestones marked the burial spots of long-forgotten faces and names from centuries past. Another chilly blast of wind nipped at their faces, flushing their cheeks. The bright ribbons of a Christmas wreath hanging on a dead child's tombstone fluttered in the wind like red flags.

A small gothic-styled building of gray stone with double doors of Art Nouveau ironwork came into view. It bore no family name, as did other mausoleums; only the number thirteen, engraved into a curved stone block above its arched entrance. Built sometime back in the late nineteenth century, the structure had become a local mystery and the subject of strange legends. Nobody in town, not even the oldest residents, knew for sure who had built the mausoleum, or whose bodies were entombed within its walls. Some people believed it was haunted, while some claimed it housed the body of a high priest who led a devil-worshipping cult.

Bradley looked down at his wristwatch. It was now ten minutes before the hour of midnight and a light snow was beginning to fall, turning the bare branches of the trees and the tops of the tombstones ghostly-white.

"It's almost time," he said as he climbed up the four stone steps leading to the front of the mausoleum. "I hope you aren't going to chicken out on me."

Carly reluctantly joined her boyfriend, continuously looking over her shoulders to ensure that no one was following them. "This is absolutely ridiculous," she stated. "And I'm freezing to death on top of everything!"

"Shhh," Bradley held his pointed index finger in front of his mouth and nose. He whispered, "I think I hear footsteps."

Carly's face went pale and she quickly turned around to see if anyone was coming. She appeared to be ready to make a run for it

"Oh, never mind," Bradley teased with a stupid grin on his face. "Must have just been one of those headless ghosts wandering around looking for its lost head." He added a moaning ghost sound.

"You asshole," Carly muttered, sounding clearly unamused. She shook her head in mock disgust at her boyfriend. She found his childish antics to be most annoying; yet, at the same time, she was enamored by his boyish charms, which she found irresistible.

Bradley let out one of his "deranged mad scientist laughs" as Carly liked to call them. Teasing his girlfriend was a favorite pastime for him. He again gazed down at his wristwatch and announced that it would be midnight in less than one minute. He began counting down the seconds, and at the stroke of twelve, as a church bell echoed in the distance to signal the start of Midnight Mass, he pounded thirteen times upon the iron door with his fist.

"Hey! Mister Death!" he called out. "You in there? We want to know, who's going to be the next one pushing up daisies in this graveyard of yours? Come on and tell us. We're waiting."

Carly sighed and rolled her eyes. She felt ridiculous being a party to this nonsense and was more than anxious for this ordeal to reach its conclusion so she could return to the comfort of her parent's house, warm her hands by the fireplace, and enjoy a nice cup of eggnog. She loved spending time with Bradley, but she was now regretting accompanying him to the cemetery.

What a crappy way to spend a Christmas Eve, she thought.

And then a strange voice that possessed an unearthly quality to it whispered from within the darkness beyond the mausoleum doors, "Bradley Beauregard is next."

A chill colder than the wind in the graveyard swept through Carly's body; she felt the blood in her veins suddenly turn to ice. With her eyes bugging out in disbelief, she turned to look at her boyfriend, whose face was cloaked by a look of shock. And then, much to her horror, the iron doors of mausoleum thirteen began to creak and squeak and slowly open right before her.

Terror surged through Carly's body like a burning electrical charge and she let out a blood-curdling scream. Without hesitation, she turned and took off running pell-mell like the proverbial bat out of hell. Within a matter of seconds she was out of sight, leaving behind only a trail of footprints in the thin dusting of freshly fallen snow that clung to the ground.

The mausoleum doors opened wide, revealing Bradley's best friend and fellow practical joker, Fletcher. The two young men looked at each other and then burst into uncontrollable laughter.

"You should have seen the look on Carly's face before she screamed loud enough to wake the dead!" laughed Bradley with tears streaming down his cheeks. "I thought her baby blues were going to pop right out of her pretty little head when she heard you whisper my name! Oh man, that was too funny! But, Fletch, you were supposed to have said *her* name, not mine."

Fletcher stopped laughing and a serious look came over his face. "That wasn't me, Brad," he explained. "I thought *you* were the one who whispered it."

Bradley smiled. "Yeah, right. You can't bullshit a bullshitter, dude. Like I don't know it was you. We've only had this joke planned out for like what… the last two months?"

"But I swear it, bro," Fletcher insisted. "It wasn't me. And if it wasn't you, then I don't know who the hell it was."

Bradley was beginning to feel annoyance with his buddy's insistence that he wasn't the ghostly whisperer when he knew for a fact that he was. He stepped inside the mausoleum and walked past Fletcher, who stood, looking dumbfounded. With his hand on his forehead like a visor and a sardonic expression on his face, Bradley roamed around in the small space, pretending to search for a third person.

"You know what, Fletch?" he said sarcastically, "I've looked high and low and I don't see anyone else inside this stiff house besides you and me. Unless it's the Invisible Man."

The sudden sound of stone grinding against stone echoed within the walls of the mausoleum and Bradley and Fletcher turned their heads in the direction from which it came. All at once, the heavy lid of the burial chamber located at the rear of the mausoleum beneath a small stained-glass window slid open. And then, like a bad dream, *it* appeared.

Hideous. Vile. Reeking of absolute evil. It was a thing of inhuman form and unearthly origin; nightmarish in its appearance and ravenous after its long sleep in the blackness of the crypt. Its yellowish, snakelike eyes fixed themselves upon Bradley's, and then the thin, blackened lips of its vertical gash of mouth pulled apart to reveal the horrific rows of glistening, tapering fangs that protruded from the upper and lower sections of its great oral cavity. They resembled grotesque stalactites and stalagmites inside a cave dripping with foul and venomous slime.

Stunned by disbelief and too horrified to speak, Bradley and Fletcher stared at the beast, unable to take their eyes off of it. They watched as it rose up higher from the crypt, darkening them with its shadow as the top of its octopus-like head nearly touched the ceiling of the mausoleum. And then, without warning, it lashed out a long tentacle with talon-like claws on the end that hooked deeply into the flesh of Bradley's throat, causing blood to shoot out through his mouth and nose. Within a split second, the creature reeled in its convulsing human prey and returned to the darkness of the crypt to feast upon its long-awaited meal. Its victim's screams echoed through the stone structure but were soon muted by the heavy lid that slid back into place, resealing itself.

Fletcher let out a blood-curdling cry of terror and ran from the mausoleum in a cold sweat as the ghostly voice whispered his name on the cold wind, over and over and over. He tripped on the four stone steps and landed face down in a pile of lifeless leaves that were the color of dried blood.

When the bright sun of Christmas morning burned away the gloomy shadows of the night before and the baying of the distant hound was replaced by the sound of wintry stillness, the gray-haired caretaker arrived for work right on time. While making his rounds through the snow-shrouded cemetery, he discovered Fletcher wandering aimlessly around mausoleum thirteen, babbling to himself incoherently.

His eyes were hollows of madness.

THE END

MEMENTO MORI (CHRISTMAS EVE)

I gazed into the silver mirrored balls
that hung from boughs of plastic evergreen.
I pondered the reflection that they showed;
a face that looked familiar, yet so strange.

The colored lights danced in the stranger's eyes
with red, green, yellow, and the saddest blue.
The melancholy Christmas memories
brought emptiness within and tears without.

I saw within the shiny orbs of glass
a child as bleak as gray December snow.
Her frozen eyes of desolation wept;
her fragile hand reached ghost-like out for mine.

Then one by one the ornaments did fall
and shatter into shards upon the floor.
Distorted, broken, lifeless like my soul
and sharp enough to slice through pulsing veins.

A silent scream was heard inside my head:
the first cut is the deepest one of all.
A crimson ocean danced inside my dreams
and washed away all traces of her pain.

MIDNIGHT SÉANCE

One by one, they arrive at the door,
old ladies wearing hats of black,
and gentlemen with their bumbershoots,
to hold a séance in the dark
on a midnight wracked by rain.

Downstairs in a parlor of green,
around a table, ornate and old,
they gather in silence, eight silhouettes.
Their anticipation steadily grows.

They join hands as the murmuring thunder
drowns out the ticking of the mantel clock.
Stealthily, the hour of shadows
creeps like a cat with velveteen paws.
Across the purple draperies, drawn,
lightning faintly gleams.

The gray-haired lady with the onyx brooch
calls out to spirits that wander the earth.
Her voice, like a cluster
of dead leaves in a gale,
asks for a rapping...
and all wait for the sign.

The seconds pass into minutes, hours;
the candlelight dances on the medium's face;
the wind in the trees moans a baleful refrain,
and only silence answers.

MY HEART-SHAPED BOX

My grief
I conceal in a heart-shaped box
alongside pressed flowers
and broken jewels
and pieces of madness
like satin-wrapped candies,
  too awful to open,
    too savory not to.

Each day
I visit my heart-shaped box
to peer at its treasures
in chambers of blood
so dark and so dreadly
like yesterdays' nightmares,
  too vile to remember,
    too grave for forgetting.

NIGHT OF THE ANOMALY

Its eyes, dark and filled with self-loathing,
stared deeply into mine, filling my soul
with mounting trepidation.
I tried to shield my vision, but found
I could not look away.

Slowly I grew incensed as the oddity
gazed fixedly, mimicking my every move
like a mime with painted eyes.
Nature's mistake, a thing I called it;
screaming my words to emotionally maim.
But still the anomaly continued to stare.

I begged the aberration
to release me from its sights;
its repulsive face I could no longer bear.
Even the most fascinating freak shows
eventually grow too painful to endure.

But it had no mercy, as I had none for it.

It stared and stared
as if daring me to look away first
confident that I wouldn't...
knowing that I couldn't.

My infuriation grew into hatred
and my guts felt sickened by the sight
of this abhorrent abnormality...
this maladjusted outcast
that never should have been born.

I wanted to murder it; to release it
from this world.

With my veins burning with rage,
I smashed the mirror
into one-thousand shards of jagged traumas,
but still the anomaly continued to stare;
monstrous, unyielding,
and with one-thousand pairs
of rage-filled eyes.

Gerri R. Gray

ODE TO THE WIDOW BISHOP

The leafy oak branch creaks
as her silent silhouette sways
ever so gently in the summer breeze.
Her tangled curls,
like spider webs of silver,
crisscross her face.

Her wretched eyes stare,
spiritless like motionless
glass eyes in a broken doll.
Their cloudy irises bewitch no more;
her wicked soul
Old Mather has put to rest.

The God-fearing eyes
savor the sight,
feasting like vultures upon a
banquet of death.
Their pious hymns pierce the night
like crows in the meadow
cackling.

ONCE UPON A LUCID DREAM

Once upon a lucid dream
when candles spun their amber webs
around my coffin, scarlet-lined
and stars fell from the sky,
I heard your footsteps cross the floor,
your heart beat like a drum.

Once upon a lucid dream
the cold hush of the endless night
screamed out with silence through the halls,
I felt your words of love
caress my ashen sleeping face,
your lips bequeathed a kiss.

Once upon a lucid dream
the swansong of the waning moon
foretold this mournful point in time,
a cloud-enshrouded eve.
We danced like spindrift on the sea,
your eyes forgave my sins.

Once upon a lucid dream
we journeyed through the looking glass
together just for old time's sake,
before you stabbed my heart.
You wrote your love-poems with my blood
and then you shut the lid.

ONE FOOT IN THE GRAVE

Dark clouds had been gathering since sunrise, slowly blotting out the sky and draping the uniformed rows of grave markers with shadows. A biting wind transformed a scatter of dead leaves into a swirling mass that spiraled into a dance of death before falling back to the earth to wait for another gust to send them airborne. It was only the second day of November – All Souls' Day – but the merciless chill of winter was already in the air.

A light drizzle began to descend from the heavens like weeping tears, darkening the mournful marble figures of religious icons and innocent lambs that stood in silent vigil over the final resting places of the dead. As the drops landed upon their heads and rolled down their cheeks, they gave the solemn stone faces the eerie appearance of crying.

Jerome Crippen paused for a moment to open his black, five hundred dollar Maglia Francesco umbrella to shield himself from the rain. He then continued on his way until he arrived at the grave of his dearly departed wife, Leonora. He had nearly forgotten where her grave was located. He had only been to it once, and that was on the day of her burial. He stood as still as the statuary around him and stared down at the small bronze grave marker before him, which bore his wife's name, along with the dates of her birth and death, the image of a cross, and the Biblical quote: WHITHER THOU GOEST, I WILL GO. He recalled that it was also raining on the day her body was laid to rest and felt strangely amused by the coincidence of it.

Leonora Crippen had died exactly one year ago on this day, leaving Jerome an enormously wealthy widower, thanks to a hefty life insurance policy that he had taken out on her several years prior to her passing. According to her death certificate, the cause of death was cardiac arrest. Despite her demise occurring at such a young age, nobody questioned the certifying physician's opinion, for Leonora was known to possess an enlarged heart resulting from years of untreated high blood pressure.

Jerome took a quick look around to determine if anyone else was in the cemetery with him. Confident that he was the sole person there – at least, the sole *living* person – he cracked a bit of a crooked grin.

"Wake up, Leonora," he said softly, almost in a singing voice, to the bronze grave marker. "It's Jerome, your loving husband. It's been one whole year now since you've been gone. Time sure flies, doesn't it, my dear? Do forgive me for not coming to visit you sooner, but you see, I've been rather busy enjoying that money your insurance policy paid out to me. I'm sure you'll be pleased to hear that you left me well provided for. In fact…" he paused to snicker, "I've been living like a king and enjoying the finest of cars, clothes, restaurants and women. Mmmm, especially the women!"

Another gust of wind swept through the cemetery and a miniature tornado of brown leaves that had dropped from the branches of some nearby trees during the previous month sailed past Jerome's Italian leather shoes. The rain felt like it had suddenly grown colder, almost icy to the touch, and was now falling harder than before, giving off a loud pitter-patter as it struck the grave marker.

"It's a bit amusing, don't you think," Jerome continued, "that you always told me I could never do anything right. Not even poison a rat. Yet, I succeeded in poisoning you, Leonora, and I did it quite well and got away with it, if you don't mind me tooting my own horn. Nobody suspected a thing. With that bad ticker of yours, they all knew you had one foot in the grave."

Jerome chuckled to himself as his mind rewound to that fateful day when, after months of careful plotting and indecision, he finally mustered up enough courage and greed to see his plan through and spike the whiskey sour drink of his unsuspecting wife with a tincture of aconite root. During his researching of poisons, he had read online that a fatal dose of this plant, which is also known as wolf's bane, results in paralysis of the heart or respiratory center, with the only post mortem signs being those of asphyxia. It sounded to him like the ideal, and least messy, way to dispose of one's unwanted spouse.

Jerome remembered, with what only can be described as a fiendish fondness, the agonized expressions on his dying wife's face as the poisoning process inched her closer to death's door, and him closer to a world of freedom made sweeter by a half-million dollar death benefit payout. Leonora had initially complained of a bad headache, followed by unpleasant bouts of nausea and diarrhea. In time, her mouth and face began to tingle and then grow numb, as did her arms and legs. A fiery sensation burned deep within her abdomen, causing her to double up in pain. Confused and sweating profusely, she struggled desperately to get a breath of air as her husband nonchalantly observed from the comfort of a tufted chair in the corner of their master bedroom, while leisurely savoring a glass of imported cognac.

And then, nearly three hours from the time that Leonora had unwittingly ingested the cleverly disguised poison, she let out one last loud and horrible gasp and her painful ordeal finally reached its deadly conclusion. Her body lay cold and still upon the heavy damask comforter of black and gold that draped the queen-size bed. Her pink peignoir was brown and sodden with vomit, and her lifeless eyes wide open and staring accusingly at her murderer.

A rumble of thunder sounded in the distance and Jerome looked up at the sky. It had formed into an ominous patchwork of gray, dark green and black, illuminated by random flashes of lightning.

"Well, my dear," Jerome sighed as he returned his gaze to his deceased wife's grave marker. "I believe the time has come for me to bid you farewell. Go back to sleep now, Leonora."

He turned and started to walk away. But then, for some unexplainable reason, an odd urge overcame him. He stopped and bent down to snatch up a rain-soaked wreath from a nearby burial plot. He then made his way back to Leonora's grave with the wreath in his hand and tossed it onto the grassy ground that covered her remains. After blowing her a mocking kiss, he uttered, "I'll see you around."

Suddenly, with a loud explosive boom, a jagged bolt of blinding lightning struck Leonora's bronze marker and shook the ground. It instantly knocked Jerome off his feet and the costly umbrella from out of his hand. He flew backwards and landed on his backside atop the wet and sticky ground that had been turned to sludge by the rain. His dropped umbrella was lifted up by a howling gust of wind and carried off before he could grab onto its curved cherry wood handle.

"Damn it!" he cursed.

As he struggled to free himself from the grip of the earthy-smelling muck, the unthinkable happened.

Like a scene from out of a horror film, or perhaps from the darkest of nightmares, the ground in front of Leonora's grave marker began to tremble until a small fissure appeared, and from out of it emerged the foul and rotting limb of a woman. Its purplish hand turned in Jerome's direction and slowly opened like a blossoming nightshade.

Paralyzed by abysmal horror, Jerome recognized the gold rings on one of the corpse's fingers. They were Leonora's bridal set. He felt a scream rise up in his numb throat. But before it could exit his mouth, Leonora's bony, claw-like hand wrapped itself around his right ankle and began dragging him toward her grave.

Jerome's scream finally found its way out but was drowned out by another deafening crash of thunder. He fought desperately to free himself from the dead woman's powerful clutch, but her supernatural-infused strength won out.

The corpse had pulled Jerome's leg calf-deep into the grave when, all at once, he felt the terrifying sensation of teeth chewing on his ankle. Deeper and deeper into his bone they gnawed. The pain was unbearable and unlike anything he had ever experienced. He continued to struggle, and he bellowed out a series of hair-raising man-shrieks that reverberated in all directions, ricocheting off of tombstones and statues and the walls of mausoleums. The pain was tantamount to the most horrendous of torture and Jerome found himself drifting in and out of consciousness until the agony was mercifully supplanted by a numbness that raced up the entire length of his leg.

At last he was able to free himself from the hellish hole that had swallowed him alive. He yanked his limb from the muddy grave, only to discover that his right foot was gone. It had been completely chewed off and a gory hemorrhage was pouring out from the ragged stump at the bottom of his partially devoured leg.

His mind reeled from the horrendous sight and his thoughts swirled inside his brain like the dead leaves whipping in the wind around him. Soon, his vision blurred and faded to black. His body violently convulsed. The rapid-fire beating of his heart ceased, and Jerome Crippen lay lifeless at the foot of Leonora's grave, his blood staining the wet blades of dormant grass a ruddy color that not even the November rain could wash away.

THE END

OPENING THE CANOPIC JAR

From a mummy's tomb his body rises,
spirit from the past, he once again lives.
Ancient pyramids dance inside his eyes;
in his kiss lies the riddle of the Sphinx.

Light from silver stars, dead a thousand years
kindles his evil that burns from within,
hungry, demonic, devouring my heart;
darkest sorceries bloom at his command.

Dream or a nightmare, I know not which.

Love's toxicity courses through his veins;
when he touches me I can feel his curse
flowing like the Nile deep into my soul;
baffled and spellbound, I cannot escape.

Hellhounds, black as jet, rip apart the night;
sandstorms escalate, blinding my vision.
Red Egyptian moon grimaces above,
blood-spilt sacrifice stains the desert sand.

God Anubis come, mummify my pain.

Gerri R. Gray

PERVADING THE EMPTY SPACES

Alone I sit breathless
on night's dark shore,
inscribing epitaphs
in the sand.

Moon-mirrored waves,
sea-thunder growling,
filling the desert wasteland
within me.

Poems of love
washed away, lost at sea,
sunken like treasure
in manta ray caves.

Pirates of passion,
fleeting obsessions,
silhouette strangers with
smiles, never speaking.

Secretly aching
for one velvet touch;
afraid one might conjure
love's fury.

POINT IN TIME

Time flies, wings of gold;
the ride ends all too soon,
leaves you old, feeling cold
like the dark side of the moon.
Life's a song, a symphony;
when it's over set it free…
it plays on forever and ever

Time heals, so they say,
time gives and takes away,
leaves no trace, empty space,
leaves no moments to embrace.
Life's a dream, a mystery
when it's over let it be…
it echoes forever and ever

This point in time
has no beginning, has no end,
but still it shines
woven from the silver threads
of all to come and all that's been.

Life time, just a rhyme,
words drifting on the breeze.
Fear and pain, tears in vain,
no more possibilities.
The minutes fade into the past
where light and shadow are steadfast;
where sorrow knows no tomorrow

Times change, rearrange

the tapestry of life.
Time will tell, this farewell
wounds my soul, cuts like a knife.
All is said and all is done;
now the ending has begun…
I'll miss you forever and ever

THE POSSESSION

She haunts me,
invades my mind
like the ghost of a dead lover
that no prayer can exorcise.

She cries, tears dripping
waters of the Nile.
I struggle in her profoundness
until I drown.

She possesses me
like a she-demon;
filling my head
with cosmic fire.

Inside me, she becomes me
and I become Farika...
I cannot escape
the pyramids
in her eyes.

PREMATURE BURIAL

Black umbrellas under the rain,
tears are shed, sympathy exchanged.
Mourners hide their faces pale,
draped in black lace veils.

The lid is closed, the casket lowered,
prayers fall on deaf ears
as to the womb of Mother Earth
my ashes are returned.

But in the rumble of the thunder
and the silence of the dirt
where flesh does rot and maggots feed,
my screams remain unheard.

Gerri R. Gray

PRIESTESS AND PENTACLE

She stands upon a seaside cliff;
 crimson velvet drapes her skin.
  Moon-bright daughter of the night,
   dancing in the wailing wind.

With braided hair of storm cloud black
 and eyes like gypsy fire aglow,
  she summons up the winds that sing
   the Druid-songs of long ago.

She raises up her shining sword
 of silver etched with many runes,
  and in the names of Lord and Lady
   conjures and draws down the moon.

She lights her censer and invokes
 the four kings of the elements;
  her sweet patchouli incense smoke
   ascending to the firmament.

A crescent moon sterling silver
 worn upon her head
  as she lights her pentagram
   with thirteen candles red.

In the center of her circle
 to the ancient gods she prays,
  skyclad 'neath the magick-bright
   quicksilver lunar rays.

She sings a song, she celebrates;
her cone of power radiates,
bright as fire and just as grand—
the universe at her command.

REFLECTIONS FROM DARK DEPTHS

'Twas on a day of gray it came to call
when flowers crumbled 'neath a shroud of white
and no birds filled the air with joyous song
and shadows took the place of sun-drenched rays.

Arriving on my threshold like a plague
it came without a warning or a sound,
an uninvited stranger cloaked in dread;
the ticking of the clock was all I heard.

Then silently it made its way inside
and scurried 'cross the Oriental rug;
the strands of dismal grayness multiplied
like omens in the starless weeping sky.

It climbed the creaking stairs and slithered past
the marble-topped credenza in the hall
until it found the room that housed my fear;
no iron locks or prayers could ward it off.

The air grew unrelenting, bitter cold
as underneath my door the vile thing crept;
it found its way into my looking glass
and from dark depths my pale reflection cried.

REMAINS

Very little of it now remains,
only odd bits and pieces
like disintegrating dream
fragments that in the morning
cling to your brain.

It's something new,
yet still the same.
Every night it traps my soul
in a web of no escape.
Sealed in walls of yellow brick,
seventeen years of teardrop stains.

Very little of it now remains,
long gone are the colors
of an era claimed by death;
the sounds and the shapes
and the patterns
all now erased.

Yet in my mind
it all remains,
cruel and void of changes,
frozen in its wedge of time,
forever a yellow brick tower;
and it's there
where I remain.

THE REVENANT

Letters of love from another life
unfold from a distant time and place.
Like eyes on yellowed photos,
staring ghostlike from the film,
invade my brain and pierce my muse.

Their pages, musty, like the shadows in my soul.
Their perfumes, long gone, like petals in winter.
Their words, like the memories they invoke,
caressed by dust, fade slowly into oblivion.
Each one a novel re-written by time.

On a wind of whispers I set them free:
each syllable a dagger in my heart,
each vowel and consonant a tombstone's epitaph.
Merged with tears, the blue ink streaks,
stinging old wounds that still ooze blood.

THE ROSARY GARROTE

From your cobwebbed pulpit
you call me a sinner,
a heathen, a whore,
an infidel...
evil.

With a self-righteous finger
you point and you judge.
Blood-stained mythologies
justify your hate.

From your throne,
gold embellished,
you brand me a witch,
a strumpet, a heretic,
abomination...
bitch.

With crosses of gold
and shards of stained glass
you slice into flesh,
you claw into minds.

But your proselytizing
I strongly defy.
Your pious hypocrisy
I deeply descry.

You hide behind vestments
and idols that weep,
persecuting the blameless,

selling illusions...
your price is a soul.

I see through your thin
sanctimonious disguise.
From the steeples on high
my ears detect your lies
reverberating.

Before your pompous altar
crucified, I proudly stand
saintly in my suffering,
hallowed in my blasphemy,
holy in my decadence.

Your prayers and execrations
are useless against me.
The fire and the brimstone
wait only for you.

SANDS OF TIME

The sands of time
flow like lava,
unremitting, destroying
all that lies within their path.
They flow deep into my mind,
decaying the dreams that
propelled my heart and
led me to the sun, so far away
from dungeons
in yellow brick castles
and smiles wrought by woe.

The sands of time
in the hourglass drop, one by one
like the tears in my cup
of English Breakfast tea
each morning and in the dead
of night.
The salty taste of sadness
turns bittersweet with regret.
The grains erode my eyes
and sculpt my reflection into
a face unrecognizable.

The sands of time
heal and hide the scars
but slice open new wounds
with their sharp-edged granules,
each bearing an image from my past.
With bleeding hands, I scoop them up,
feeling their scorpion stings,

torrid.
Shutting my eyes,
I cast them into the wind
and say good bye.

SEASON OF THE CRONE

Crone of winter's spellbound cold,
in her cauldron black are told
secrets ancient, truths and tales,
mystery her fire unveils.

Crone of wisdom, hag of changes,
Body and spirit, she rearranges.
She's the seed that sprouts from death,
transformation is her breath.

Crone of darkness, beldame wise,
look beyond her gargoyle guise.
Let her lessons teach you well:
life is but a magic spell.

SEVEN TEARS FOR EVERY SMILE

If I gave to you my withered bloom,
would you charm the rain?
If I gave you crags where shadows loom,
would you quell my pain?

If I gave to you the moon agleam,
would you be my night?
If I gave to you my darkest dream,
would you then shine bright?

Seven tears for every smile
falling down like stars;
all the while they compile
secrets in a jar.

If I gave to you a poet's soul,
what words would you pen?
Would they be an endless hole
time and time again?

If I gave to you a looking glass,
whose face would it show
in its cracked and faded lines?
What would it bestow?

Seven tears for every smile
stretching far and wide…
or just one kiss to warm the frozen
emptiness inside?

SHADOWFEST

Moon of magic;
blood for fertility;
Druid fires blazing bright;
spirits roaming;
wail of the banshee;
otherworld shadows
 drape the night.

Raven soaring;
wings of sorcery;
eyes like darkest midnight
  gaze,
Silhouettes gather;
moment of mysteries;
born again the ancient ways.

THE SHADOWS TASTE YOUR FEAR

There are things far worse
than death to fear
and realities in this world
more terrifying
than the darkest of nightmares.

When the cold black night
entombs the day,
pray not that you shall ever know
what unspeakable things exist behind
the shadows on your wall.

SILENT STRANGER

Silent stranger, high you stand
above the rocky cliffs of gray
where ocean waves unceasingly pound,
unapologetic.
You fill me with questions
that have no answers, only desolation.

Ghostly shadow-forms you sketch
upon the endless shoreline
shrouded thick in silvery mist;
and swallowed by the tides.
You stroll the lonely beaches
and leave no footprints in the sand.

Your faceless presence haunts my mind
like bells of phantom vessels
ringing out in the midnight fog.
Your soul resides in moon-kissed wings
of stormbound seabirds
and tempests that rage.

Ocean child, you call to the sea
with voices from the past.
Your words, in bottles, float away;
your starfish eyes bewitch me.
I see reflections of Atlantis
shimmering in your eyes.

SINISTER CONSEQUENCES

His appearance was a mystery, if not a complete impossibility. There was no human way he could have gotten in. The cell door was locked tight and carefully guarded by a night duty officer.

"Wake up, Martha," he whispered in a voice as soft as velvet. "I've come to make a deal with you."

Martha awoke from her restless sleep and sat up. "Is it time?" she asked in a fragile sounding voice. Dread clung to her words like drops of morning dew.

The shadowless man with the black Van Dyke beard smiled at her. His eyes were like those of a raven. "It is time for you to make a choice regarding your life," he replied.

"A choice regarding my life?" Martha asked, confused and rubbing the sleep away from her eyes. "My execution is in the morning. I'm a dead woman in just a matter of time."

"Six hours, six minutes, and six seconds to be exact," said the man.

Martha was puzzled. She had never seen this man before but yet something about him seemed familiar. She couldn't quite figure him out. "Who are you?" she asked, pulling her state-issued sheet up to her collarbone in order to cover her chest. "How did you get past the guards and inside my cell?"

"I think you know who I am, Martha. You've always known me, and I've always known you. I was there when you murdered your husband for the insurance money, hacked his body into little pieces, and buried them in the flower garden behind the house. I must say I was quite proud of the way in which you plotted it and carried it out. And you almost got away with it too. It's such a pity that you didn't. I was really rooting for you."

"Are you… Death?" Martha asked, cowering with fear.

"Not at all, my dear," the man replied in a cheerful sounding voice. "I'm your personal demon."

"My personal demon? I never knew I had one," said Martha, sounding rather surprised.

"Everybody has one," replied the demon, stroking his beard. "We're assigned to you at the moment of your birth."

Martha shook her head in disbelief. "I must be dreaming," she said. "This can't be!"

The demon gave a small laugh and then assured her that she was quite awake and that he was quite real. "As I've told you before," he explained, "I've come to offer you a choice: Life in another place and time, or death in the gas chamber. The choice is up to you, Martha. What do you have to lose?"

Martha pondered the demon's offer for a few moments and then nodded her head in agreement. "All right then. I'll choose the first option. What do I have to do to seal the deal?"

"Just sign your name, in blood, of course, in the Master's Black Book and the exchange will be made." From out of thin air, a large book with a black leather-bound cover materialized in his hand; a long silver pin appeared in the other.

"The exchange?" Martha asked, feeling a trifle bit puzzled.

"Life in another place and time in exchange for your soul," the demon answered. "Now, don't look so alarmed. You're a smart girl, so you must be aware that the murder you committed has already guaranteed your soul eternal damnation. So you have nothing really to lose by a friendly little transaction." And with that being said, he smiled once again. He appeared quite confident that Martha's fear of death and desire to live would persuade her to give him what he had come for. "My time grows short, Martha. Do we have a deal or not?"

The very idea of selling her soul to the Devil filled Martha with an uneasy feeling, but the demon did have a good point she told herself, and like he had said, she really had nothing to lose at this point. His offer was her only chance of escaping the frightening fate that awaited her in the prison's gas chamber.

"Okay. It's a deal," she said, nodding her head.

The demon handed Martha the silver pin and then held the book open for her to sign. She shut her eyes and pricked the tip of her left thumb with the sharp end of the pin. The stinging sensation that ensued caused her to let out a small gasp. She opened her eyes and squeezed out a droplet of blood from the tiny puncture wound, dipped the tip of the pin into it, and then used it like a fountain pen to scrawl her name in the infernal book.

All at once there came a thunderous rumbling sound from somewhere deep within the earth and then Martha felt as if she had awakened from a long dream. She found herself alone and in a strange room that smelled like the inside of a barn. The cobble-stoned floor beneath her feet was strewn with straw and in the corner was a small bed made from bundles of straw tied together. Above the bed was a tiny rectangular window that was letting in the first rays of morning sunlight.

Curious as to where she was, Martha climbed onto the bed and peered out the window to take a look. To her amazement, she saw a small village of Colonial-styled houses and unpaved roads upon which hordes of people dressed in what appeared to be seventeenth century attire walked, and men on horses pulling carts rode. Oddly, they were all traveling in the same direction and within a short matter of time had gathered in the village square, chattering and laughing.

As Martha watched the size of the crowd swell from a few dozen to several hundred, she began to laugh. "I tricked the demon and his master!" she said out loud, feeling quite proud of her cunning. "I'm in another place and time now. I haven't taken anyone's life. There's been no murder of my husband, which means I've not committed a sin. I'm an innocent woman now, so my soul is safe from eternal damnation. My name won't even appear in the Devil's book until hundreds of years from now! I beat him and that demon of his at their own game! I'm free!"

The sudden rattling of metal keys popped Martha's musing like a balloon. Her mind immediately surged with fear that this new place and time she had been transported to was nothing but a dream and at any moment she would open her eyes to find herself back in her prison cell with the priest and warden ready to escort her to the gas chamber.

The seconds seemed to drag into hours as the door was being unlocked from the other side. And then it slowly opened. To Martha's horror, there stood her husband, dressed in odd attire. He wore a full-sleeved blouse, over which was a waistcoat and a doublet. Below that was a pair of breeches fastened at each of his knees with a garter. The lower half of his legs were covered by cotton stockings and high-topped boots with turnovers, and upon his head he wore a large felt hat with a wide brim. He stared her in the eyes.

"William!" she screamed in disbelief as she backed up from him, fearfully. "Oh my god! You're alive!"

The man stood in silence for a few moments before speaking. "Beggin' your pardon, Miss, but thou must have me confused with someone else. Me name's Elias, not William. And I should hope to be alive!"

Martha carefully studied the contours of the man's face. The resemblance to her dead husband was uncanny. She breathed a sigh of relief and then asked him, "Could you please tell me where I am and what is today's date?"

The man gave her a queer look and then replied with a grin. "Why, surely thou must know. In the jail of Salem Village is thee, on the twenty-second morn of September in the year of our Lord, sixteen hundred and ninety-two... the day thou hangs on Gallows Hill for the crime of consorting with the Devil!"

THE END

Gerri R. Gray

SISTER-CIRCLE

I had been an only child,
once I was a lonely child
wishing for a sister-friend to share
my gypsy dreams.

And then there came a lady of herbs,
  a Black Swan blessed with wort-cunning ways.
And then Panthere, a lady of jewels
  whose gifts are her art
  and poetic phrase.
And then a third there came to be –
  a child of Saturn and Earth as me.

And now the sister-circle widens;
in its light our spirit rises.
Shadows grow a bit less dark
as we heal and strengthen.

I had been an only child,
once I was a lonely child
wishing for a sister-friend –
and
now I have many.

SLEEP NOW

Sleep now, sweet child,
Mother Earth shall be your bed,
and the quicksilver moon
will caress your sleepy head.

Sleep now, dear angel,
Father Time shall keep you safe
from the gathering storms
and your eyes shall weep no more.

Sleep now in silence,
underneath a crimson rose,
in a black velvet dream
where the cruel wind never blows.

THE SPIRIT LAMP

A brass dragon spirit lamp
within the tower glows;
outside, a storming night
calls to the raven
with wings upon the wind.

She lights a fire to quell the cold
and draw the drapes
crushed velvet
royal blue.

The spirit lamp
cast flickering shadows
upon her chamber's stony walls.
With silent eyes she gazes
as fateful shapes appear.

They dance.
They shimmer.
They haunt her mind
like ghost-white specters
of the night.

She closes her eyes
and escapes into memories
of lovers and places
beyond the tower walls.
She struggles
to retain their clarity
as the hands of time
grow them vague.

Down and dim the spirit lamp burns,
its flame fading from sight.
The storm rages like a ghastly curse
without
and within.

THE SPIRIT LAMP (continued)

She sits before a broken mirror...
her reflection from another
place and time.
She slowly brushes
her cascading hair,
darker than midnight...
and black as the raven's eyes.

Her face recedes
gray and ghostly.
She knows the hour
of his thirst
approaches.

His footsteps echo
on the tower stairs,
and a fragile cobweb trembles
in a corner high and lonely.

Increasingly louder they grow
with each horrific step
as does the dread
all too familiar to her heart.

The lion's head door knob
slowly turns, the rusted hinges
let out a shriek.
The brass dragon spirit lamp
flickers in vain,
then succumbs to the darkness,
as does she.

STAR CHILDE

Star Childe in the indigo night,
misty-sweet with frankincense smoke.
His hooded robe flows soft and white,
he kneels in shadows of gnarled oak.

Magus of the olden ways,
he radiates with power.
Beneath a rising moon ablaze
he blossoms like a flower.

Star Childe glowing brighter
than the universe above,
casts enchantments on my heart
and weaves a spell of love.

In his ancient eyes I see
galaxies of dream-montage,
and with one kiss my mind transforms
into mirth and mirage.

When silver is the moon so round,
he rises nude on hoofed feet
just like a bearded Centaur crowned
with nettles, thorns, and petals sweet.

Star Childe in the raging dawn,
misty-sweet with golden beams.
Like a river of stars he flows
into my sea of dreams.

ELLA ROSA

STORM WARNING

Today I heard the wind call out your name,
I turned to look but nothing stayed the same.
A withered leaf swirled ghost-like in the lane.

Bitter grew the air as the blackness loomed
upon the far horizon draped in gloom,
emerging like a demon from its womb.

Today I felt the cold rain hit my face
and from its wrath there was no hiding place:
reflections of a life that I'd misplaced.

I thought I saw your shadow, heard your sigh
within my ear as storm clouds gathered high:
the thunder rumbled grimly to deny.

A tempest surged like madness in my mind
sabotaging everything it could find,
it left me feeling splintered and resigned.

Today, again, I wondered: could I be free?
I watched the whirling storm move out to sea
and gathered up the wind-swept bits of me.

Today I shut my eyes and I could see.

STRANGERS AMONG US

They streak the desert sky with light,
  they make the mountains quiver.
They walk the city streets at night
  with glowing eyes of silver.

Deep in dripping caves of gloom
  they lie asleep 'til sunset,
wrapped in crystalline cocoons
  like weird transforming insects.

They eat the minds of sleeping men,
  devour their screaming dreams and then
they disappear without a trace;
  invaders of the human race.

They look like you,
  they look like me;
They make it hard for us to see
  illusions from reality.

Gerri R. Gray

SUNDAY AFTERNOON

Sunday afternoon, I close my eyes
drowning in tears, stained
like church windows.
Dancing naked in grass,
darkest meadow green and high.
Feel the moment
wrap around my soul.

Fragments of white crystal mind
shatter into dreamless pieces,
scattered like stars across
a colorless universe.

Sunday afternoon, day turns
into silent shadows, wilting
like flower children
crushed and bleeding
under leather gloved hands.

Stench of war sours
the air. Blood of man
flows like polluted rivers,
forming cesspools
of society.

THE TAPHOPHILE

I am a taphophile and have been for many years. Perhaps you've heard of the word before… perhaps not. At any rate, it literally means "a person with a fondness for, or is attracted to, graves, tombs, and/or funerals." As a taphophile, one of my passions is visiting old cemeteries to photograph the tombstones, mausoleums, and funerary statues. I realize there are some who would regard my unusual interest as a rather morbid pastime. But that's only because they don't see the *bella morte* – the beauty of death – through the same eyes as mine.

It was in the early springtime, on the kind of day when little islands of melting snow cling to the awakening hills, and winter's slowly dying breath lingers stubbornly in the air, that the cemetery known as Primrose Hill called out to me. I parked my van on a patch of level ground, alongside the gravel-covered road that wound its way past the graves of corpses from another century and set off on foot with my digital camera in hand.

With the exception of the occasional cawing of an unseen crow and the crunching sound my boot heels made as I walked upon the loose aggregation of crushed stones, the place was blanketed in a peaceful silence. There appeared not to be another soul around, which was fine by me since I'm hardly what you'd call a 'people person.' Solitude is one of the things that I cherish dearly, yet one of the things I never seem to get enough of.

For a small-town cemetery, Primrose Hill was fairly large and bordered on three sides by the wilds of a sprawling forest preserve. Its oldest section dated back to the mid-nineteenth century and was dotted with weathered gravestones into which were engraved poetic epitaphs. Mausoleums with Gothic, Grecian and Art Nouveau architectural details sprung up from the hillsides, and larger-than-life statues – some with missing hands, and others, entire arms – stood like motionless sentinels with perpetually mourning faces.

After about fifteen minutes of walking about and snapping pictures, I came upon a small mausoleum situated alongside the main road. My eyes were instantly drawn to its ironwork doors, which featured an elaborate Egyptian-themed design. Unlike the chained and padlocked doors of all the other mausoleums I had seen and photographed, these were unlocked and stood invitingly ajar. My taphophile heart jumped for joy!

I had photographed many mausoleums in the past, but never their interiors. The unlocked doors of this one were beckoning me to enter, and I was unable to resist the temptation. The unexpected and rare opportunity to photograph one from the inside was too good not to take advantage of.

I took a quick look around to ensure that no one was watching, and then began to ascend the mausoleum's slab-like steps that lead up to its entrance. But just as I reached the top, the crunching sound of tires on the gravel road stopped me in my tracks. *Damn it!* I cursed to myself, dreading that it was the cemetery's caretaker in his rickety, white Ford pickup truck, for I'd had a few unpleasant run-ins with him in the past. A cantankerous old louse whose mouth bore a slight droop from a long-ago stroke, he had made it quite clear that his feelings for "morbid weirdos" like me were anything but amicable. All I needed was for him to accuse me of breaking into a mausoleum and call the police, which I had little doubt he would do, given the opportunity.

The vehicle turned out to be a black, late model Corvette, and I exhaled a sigh of relief. As it slowly crept past me, the driver – a dark-haired man in his mid-to-late thirties – turned his head in my direction and flashed me an overtly flirtatious smile. I found it to be a rather odd thing, considering he had an attractive, blonde-haired woman sitting right next to him. She stared straight ahead at the road, avoiding eye contact.

After the car disappeared from sight, I took a peek through the open doors of the mausoleum and then ventured inside with camera in hand. Curiously, the air within the mausoleum was noticeably colder than the air outside. The walls at each side contained several crypts, and on the back wall a colorful stained-glass window depicting a winged hourglass encircled by a wreath of lilies radiated in the sunlight.

I had taken at least a dozen pictures when, all of a sudden, a bone-chilling gust scattered some dead leaves across the marble floor. I was sure I heard, within the moaning of the wind, a faint and ghostly voice telling me to go home. I chuckled at my over-active imagination and then proceeded to snap a few more photos, including some "selfies." With my curiosity satisfied, I exited the mausoleum, shutting the doors behind me. I then continued strolling through Primrose Hill, stopping periodically to capture with my camera a particularly interesting gravestone or the haunting beauty of a weeping stone cherub.

I was photographing vistas from the top of a pine-covered hill at the other end of the cemetery, when my ears were suddenly filled with loud rock and roll music. I instinctively turned my head in the direction from which the sound came and observed the same black Corvette that had passed by me earlier pull over to the side of the road at the bottom of the hill. It sat there for several minutes with its engine running and radio blaring before the door on the passenger's side flew open and the blonde-haired woman bolted from the vehicle, screaming wildly on the top of her lungs. The driver's door swung open and the dark-haired man jumped from the car and took off after the fleeing woman. He quickly caught up to her, and then, to my absolute horror, I watched him place what appeared to be a long, white extension cord around her neck and began violently choking her with it. She struggled for a bit, kicking and clawing at her assailant, and finally collapsed upon the ground. The man stuffed the cord into the front pocket of his jacket and then started dragging the woman's limp body into the nearby woods.

I could scarcely believe what my eyes had just witnessed. It was surreal, to say the least!

Terrified, I took off running as fast as I could, my feet stumbling over grave markers and tree roots that protruded from the earth like gnarled fingers. All I could think about was getting out of Primrose Hill as fast as possible and notifying the police. I scolded myself for not getting the license plate number of the Corvette, even though I was too far away to make it out clearly.

And then I regretted not heeding the warning of the ghostly voice in the mausoleum. I was convinced beyond the shadow of a doubt that it was portentous in its nature. *Oh, why didn't I listen to it and leave when I had the chance?* I grilled myself.

I had been running for quite some time and felt as if I were going in circles. I then realized I had managed to get myself lost. I paused to catch my breath and collect my thoughts by a granite sarcophagus guarded by a large metallic angel whose copper alloys had oxidized to blue-green. My lungs felt as though they were on fire and a cold sweat beaded up on my forehead. I ordered my trembling body to calm down and tried to convince myself that everything would be all right; I would surely find my way back to my van, sooner or later. I gazed around and was relieved to see no sign of the Corvette. I took a deep breath and then once again broke into a run.

The road eventually forked, and I had to choose whether to go left or to go right. A gut feeling – call it 'woman's intuition' if you like – prompted me to go right, so I did. I spotted the mausoleum with the unlocked doors just up the road and knew I was heading in the right direction.

"Yes!" I shouted with a burst of glee.

I began to run faster and, within a few minutes, my parked van came into view. Nothing could have been a more welcome sight at that moment! I suddenly felt overwhelmed by a flood of emotions, and tears welled up in my eyes.

I unlocked the door to my van, rushed to get in, and then quickly locked the door. With my hand shaking, I inserted the key into the ignition and turned it. Like a scene out of some godforsaken horror movie, the van wouldn't start. *This can't be happening.*

"God damn it!" I screamed at the instrument panel. I tried to start it again, but the engine still refused to turn over. And then I spied the black Corvette ominously approaching. A wave of dread washed over me. The car pulled up alongside of me and the driver got out and casually walked up to my door. I instantly recognized him as the man who had strangled the blonde. He rapped on my rolled-up window with his knuckles and asked if I were in need of any help. *Maybe he doesn't know that I saw what he did to that girl,* I said to myself, trying to calm the terror that was rising up from the pit of my stomach. I turned to him and forced a smile upon my lips. "I'm fine, thank you," I lied, trying my utmost not to sound as though I had just witnessed a cold-blooded murder. "I'm just waiting for my husband." I gazed down at the watch on my wrist and then turned back to the man who was peering at me through the window. "He should be showing up any minute now."

"Oh, you don't say?" he asked me. The tone of his voice told me he didn't believe my story. (I guess I never was very good at telling fibs.) A frightful scowl contorted the muscles of his face. His watery blue eyes glared at mine, filling me with uneasiness. They were cold and empty eyes, like those of a predatory animal... and he was stalking his prey.

I nodded my head, straining my face to maintain the smile. Panic was clawing at my insides, but I had to keep a calm exterior. If I exhibited even the slightest sign of fear, he would surely know that I had witnessed his unspeakable crime. He turned and began to walk back to the Corvette. I exhaled a sigh of relief. However, it proved to be premature, as he stopped after taking a few steps and then returned to my window. His face was now aglow with an eerie, feigned smile, as though he had slipped on a friendly-looking mask to gain my trust while he had his back to me.

"You wouldn't, by any chance, be lying through your teeth to me, would you?" he inquired.

"No," I lied through my teeth. "Of course not. I have no reason to do that."

The smile on his face dissolved back into a snarl. His eyes turned menacing. "Women are always lying! It's what bitches do best!" he yelled in an insane voice. "Filthy lying whores! Every fucking one of them! And you're no different from the rest!"

"My husband is going to be arriving any second now!" I reiterated, hoping it would prompt the man to leave. But it soon became apparent to me that he had no such intention.

He went over to his car, opened the door on the passenger side, and retrieved something from the glove compartment. To my horror, he then returned to the spot where I was parked. His right hand was wrapped tightly around the handle of a black, steel, expandable baton. I blared my horn, but it didn't faze him in the least. With his teeth clenched, he swung the baton against my window, taking out a small chip of glass. I frantically pumped the gas pedal and tried the ignition key again and again, but the van stubbornly refused to start. There came another swing of the baton and a crack resembling a spider's web fanned out with a loud thud. Shielding my face with the back of my hand, I let out a scream, and then another swing of the baton completely shattered the window, showering me with pieces of broken glass. I scrambled across to the passenger seat as he pulled up on the lock and opened my door. Like a wild animal, he lunged at me, but I managed to open the passenger door in the nick of time and fled from the van into the adjoining woods.

Branches and prickly weeds scratched at my face and body as I ran like a doe from a hunter. The forest grew denser and darker, and I felt like a small, helpless creature being swallowed alive by some giant monster with a voracious appetite.

I don't know for how long I had been running. It felt like an eternity. My leg muscles were on fire with pain, my stomach was cramping up, and my pounding heart felt ready to burst. The terror-stricken little voice in my head told me I had to keep moving, but my fatigued body demanded a rest. I paused for a brief bit to catch my breath, all the while keeping my ears alert to the sound of the killer's approaching footsteps. But all I heard was a loud droning coming from beyond a fern-guarded outcropping of low rocks. I don't know why, but I felt strangely compelled to follow the sound, as if my will was no longer my own.

The buzzing grew louder as I climbed over the ferns and rocks, until, all at once, it became intense, filling my ears with the rapid beating of a thousand swarming wings. Gazing down, my eyes were met by the sickening sight of six dead bodies. The maggot-infested carcasses all appeared to be female and were arranged in disturbingly obscene poses. Some were partially clothed, while others were completely nude. All had been grotesquely mutilated. Hordes of flies and bees and other winged insects crawled upon them, feasting on their remains, while others circled in the air above them. The eyes of one of the fresher-looking corpses were being pecked at and consumed by a trio of contentious crows.

My brain reeled, and my stomach churned. I turned away and vomited onto a carpet of moss and fallen branches. The spell was broken and once again I sprinted as if my feet had suddenly sprouted wings. Through a thicket of trees, I could make out the shape of a building in the near distance. I ran towards it. However, as I drew nearer to the structure and realized that it was nothing more than the derelict ruins of an old chapel that had long ago been abandoned and boarded-up, my short-lived spark of optimism extinguished like a burning wick in a rain storm.

Part of the wall at the rear of the chapel had crumbled away over the years, leaving a small opening at the bottom that was partially obscured by a clump of dead, thorny briars and brambles. It appeared to be large enough for me to squeeze my body through it, so I decided to venture inside and hide from the killer that was pursuing me. And then a thought ran through my mind. *Perhaps I'd get lucky and find something within the building that I could arm myself with should he discover my whereabouts.* Using a thick stick as a primitive tool to keep the thorny branches at bay, I crouched down in front of the opening and then crawled through it on my hands and knees, taking care not to damage my camera. My back, on the other hand, did not make it through unscathed. A jagged piece of stone protruding like a stalactite from the upper part of the hole ripped through the material of my jacket, slicing open my flesh from between my shoulder blades down to the small of my back. I clenched my teeth and forced the pain out of my mind, daring not to make a sound in case the killer was within earshot.

I was now inside the chapel, which was lit by hazy rays of sunlight that beamed through random holes where the rotting roof had fallen away. I stood up and, with my hands, dusted off the dirt and webs from my clothes. I gazed around at my surroundings, keeping my eyes peeled for anything with potential as a weapon for self-defense. The floor was buried under years of dirt, bits of broken plaster, and splintered wood. Filthy wooden pews, some broken, were strewn about, and a rust-encrusted, wrought iron chandelier that had fallen victim to a crumbling ceiling and gravity, sat idly on the ground, enshrouded by long-forsaken spider webs, thick with dust.

I made my way across the rubble to the altar, hoping to find some heavy brass candlesticks that could be used to bash a man's skull in, but there were none to be found. Upon the altar were nothing but a dusty taper candle and an equally dusty box containing a single wooden match. Looking around, my eyes caught sight of a large, round object on the floor, which I estimated to be roughly six inches in diameter. Using my foot, I cleared
away the debris around it and discovered it was the iron pull ring of a trap door in the floor. I grabbed onto it and lifted up the door. Ten stone steps leading down to what appeared to be an ancient crypt came into view. At the bottom, a large rat scurried by and vanished into a veil of shadows.

My instincts were strongly advising me not to go down there. But rats or no rats, I felt I was really left with no other alternative. In the likely event that the killer came looking for me in the chapel, the underground chamber afforded me the best, and only, hiding spot. It was my one and only chance to survive.

I struck the match against the side of the altar. No flame... not even a spark. On the fourth try, its sulfur head ignited, and I lit the candle in preparation for my descent into whatever hell awaited me below. I began to climb down the steps, shutting the trap door over my head. The dim glow of the candle's flame cast flickering shadows upon the walls of stone below and gave the room the ambiance of a medieval dungeon. The crypt itself was long and narrow, abundant with cobwebs, and deathly silent except for the slow and steady sound of dripping water. On the cobblestone floor, in the center of the dank, subterranean chamber, sat six dust-covered, wooden coffins. They were rather plain in appearance and looked to be extremely old.

On any other given day, I would not have hesitated to raise their lids and capture some postmortem shots with my camera. However, I couldn't risk the sound of squeaking coffin hinges giving away my hiding spot in case the killer was lurking nearby.

The flame on my candle suddenly sputtered and then met its demise, and I was swallowed up by the immediate ensuing darkness. I stood motionless. Waiting. Listening.

Drip...

Drip...

Drip...

And then the sound of something scratching at wood came from somewhere in the black void that surrounded me like a sea of pitch. It stopped for a few moments and then continued; only this time it was louder than before. My thoughts flashed back to the not-so-small rat I had seen dart by earlier and I felt a panic attack brewing. My fear of rats started in childhood after watching the 1970's film, *Willard*, and far outweighed my other phobias, which were spiders and heights. I listened with dread in my heart as the sounds of tiny claws intensified. Soon, they were joined by other scratching noises coming from different locations around me in the dark. I envisioned myself surrounded by an army of hideous, gigantic rats. I struggled furiously to restrain myself from freaking out.

Suddenly, I felt something sharp, like long fingernails, pierce the flesh of my right upper arm. The pain was searing and caused me to scream and drop my camera. It hit the stone floor with a crash and the impact activated the flash and the fingernails immediately withdrew from my arm. The bright light that momentarily illuminated the confines of the crypt unveiled a terrifying scene that seemed too nightmarish to be real. Yet it *was* real.

Standing around me were half a dozen corpses in varying states of decomposition. Rotting faces, some more skull than flesh, gazed upon me hungrily from all directions. To my ultimate horror, these things that should have been dead and lying still in their graves were alive as if by some power most unholy.

The light from the flash died away after a second and the inky blackness once again consumed the crypt. I could hear the horrible breathing noises emitted by those undead things, followed by the sounds of their dragging feet moving closer to the spot where I stood, paralyzed from head to toe with fear. My blood instantly turned to ice in my veins. I let out another scream that was loud enough to wake up the dead; however, it was quite
evident that they already were. I turned to flee, but my escape from the crypt was impeded by the long fingernails of other hellish hands that dug into my flesh like razor-sharp talons. My screams ricocheted off the damp walls of stone and echoed throughout the crypt and the chapel above as I struggled to free myself.

At last I managed to break away from the living dead things, which were now emitting high-pitched shrieking noises that were as horrible sounding as they were inhuman. Rushing towards the steps that lead out of this chamber of horror, I knocked one or two of the foul creatures onto the ground. The sound of their brittle bones cracking and their skulls shattering assaulted my ears. It was like a sound straight out of a nightmare… a sound that will never leave my memory for as long as I continue to live.

Running as quickly as humanly possible, I made it half the way up the stairs before tripping. I fell facedown, twisting my left ankle and banging up my knees and forearms in the process. Patches of my skin had been shredded by the rough texture of the stones, and from my stinging wounds my blood dribbled out, exciting those abominable things that I could hear getting closer. My heart was thumping furiously in my chest. I thought at any

given moment it might burst and that would be the end of me. A quick death would certainly be preferable to being devoured alive by these decaying things that, by all accounts, should have been dead; yet, in defiance of the laws of the natural world, were not.

All at once, I felt a skeletal hand wrap its bony fingers around my injured ankle and attempt to drag me back down into the crypt. A surge of panic-driven adrenaline provided me with the strength needed to kick myself free from the monstrous grip. Ignoring the pain from my injuries, I picked myself up and made a mad dash the rest of the way up the stairs and out of the ruins of the abandoned chapel.

My ankle was rapidly swelling up and the pain was growing in its intensity. However, I dared not stop to rest. I had to keep running, no matter how great the pain. Through the leafless branches of tangled trees and shrubs, I could see glimpses of the winding road up ahead. I then heard the sound of tires rolling over loose gravel and could make out a vehicle. It was the white Ford pickup truck belonging to the cemetery's caretaker. *Oh, thank God*, I thought, and then almost chuckled out loud. Never in my wildest dreams would I have thought the day would come when I'd be pleased to see that man. But that day was today. As I continued to run towards the road, I began to shout for help and wave my arms wildly, hoping that he would hear my voice or see me and stop.

And then, I felt something slip around my neck, stopping me in my tracks and cutting off my supply of air. Without seeing it, and even before clutching at it in an attempt to rip it away from my throat, I knew right away it was the killer's garrote. As I fought tooth and nail to regain my freedom, as well as my breath, I could see, through the branches, the white pickup truck drive past and disappear around the bend. My hope for being rescued vanished right along with it.

"You didn't really think you were going to get away from me that easily, did you, bitch?" came a man's raspy voice from behind me. It was void of humanity and filled with a cruelness that ran deep. "Stop struggling and just accept your fate," he demanded. "Don't you understand? You have to die. I can't leave any witnesses."

I was certain that my demise was but minutes away and I became panic-stricken. However, with my throat being crushed, I was unable to scream or even plead for my life. A frightful gurgling noise was all I could manage. My heart was pounding. My vision was getting blurry. I could scarcely believe what was happening to me. It had to be a bad dream. It just *had* to be.

I had always heard that it was a common thing for death to be preceded by the flashing of one's life before their eyes. However, the only thing I could see in my mind's eye was the horrifying image of my strangled corpse decomposing in the woods, alongside the dead bodies of the madman's other victims.

Confusion and dizziness were now setting in and I found that I was rapidly losing the strength to struggle. My arms were going limp. The cord around my neck tightened and its fibers cut deeper into my flesh. I could feel my face puffing up and I somehow sensed it was turning a shade of beet red or perhaps even purple. I then heard my assailant's voice taunting me with his twisted plan to rape my corpse.

I wasn't a religious person; but, at this point, I found myself praying inside my head to God, or to anyone else who would listen, to stop my agony. I just wanted my inevitable death to be swift and mercifully bring this living nightmare to an end. I suddenly began to slip into a drowsy, almost dream-like, state and my panic melted away into a strange peacefulness. I knew my death was rapidly approaching.

My body was starting to slump to the ground when I heard the man behind me wailing out loud like a demon. He released the cord from my neck and I landed on the wet leaves that carpeted the floor of the woodland. I immediately gasped to refill my lungs with air and then coughed and panted like an overheated dog. My head was pounding with pain that was far worse than any migraine headache I had ever experienced, and it hurt like hell to swallow. But there were no words to describe how wonderful it felt to still be alive.

Just before I descended into unconsciousness, my eyes beheld the horrific sight of the six undead creatures from the chapel's crypt savagely ripping the head and limbs from the killer's torso. His blood sprayed in the air in every direction, and some of the splatter, still warm to the touch, landed in my hair and on my face. His wailing ceased, and the creatures began to feed on his bloodied body parts.

When I came to, I found myself sitting on the glass-covered front seat of my van. My dented camera was sitting on the seat beside me, and there was no sign of the black Corvette. Confusion flooded my brain. *How did I get back to my van?* I wondered. *Was it all just a horrible dream?* Nothing made any sense. I examined my throat in the rearview mirror. It was badly bruised, and a dark red mark left by the extension cord confirmed the reality of my nightmarish ordeal.

With curiosity eating away at me, I picked up my camera and switched it on. I was pleasantly surprised to find it still in working condition after having been dropped on a cobblestone floor. I set it to playback mode and scrolled through all the pictures until the last one taken was displayed on the LCD screen. It was a tilted, low-angle shot of an empty crypt.

THE END

TEARS OF STONE

Eyes of an angel
sent from on high
to weep stone tears
forever and a day.

Face of an angel,
haunted, forlorn;
no comfort sweet
can ever be her gift.

Wings of an angel,
broken and gray;
they pierce my soul
but never set me free.

Lips of an angel,
kisses for death;
of tragic lives
they whisper in the wind…

Of bright tomorrows
they speak not.

TELEPATHY

Unlock the door and
reach inside my mind
if you should feel so inclined,
if you dare...

Speak not with words aloud,
  and know my ghastly thoughts.
Look not with eyes wide open,
  and see my darkest horrors.

Listen not with curious ears,
  and hear my deepest sorrows.
Touch not my flesh with fingers,
  and feel my hellish pain.

Gerri R. Gray

THIRTEEN MINUTES PAST THE HOUR

I wake up in opaque desolation
with pieces of my hagridden sleep
fading quick to dimness uninspiring
not one angel hears my fierce prayer
I scream out words as sharp as broken glass
My throat burns, aroused by rage
I pound my fists against the air
My flesh feels a rush of fever
I think of death in November
Each time I open my eyes.

THE THIRTEENTH RUNE

Shadows of the misty moon,
whispering the thirteenth rune,
weaves a spell of waxing light
by which she does enchant the night.

Bejeweled by stars,
she sails on by,
brilliant in her silent dance;
a ritual of dark romance.

Priestess of the silver veil,
charming as the minstrel's tale,
chilling as the banshee's wail,
sacred as the Holy Grail.

TICKET TO THE UNIVERSE

Journey through the galaxy
  to all distant lands.
Sail beyond the seven seas;
  let your mind expand.

Climb aboard a ship of dreams
  and fly high above.
Hitch a ride on a time machine
  back to the Summer of Love.

See the future, see the past;
  open up your Third Eye.
The truth we seek is clear at last;
  we can fly if we try.

Got a ticket to the universe
  and I'm feeling so fine.
Got a ticket to the universe...
  universal mind.

TODAY I FEEL

Today I feel like shards of glass,
mirrored pieces disarranged,
like Sylvia Plath, her head in the oven,
never speaking to God again.
Gone my treasures, bright and shining;
vacant now my chest of hope.
Pierced with silence, noblest of hearts;
no parting consolation gifts.

Today I feel like mist and shadow,
disconnected, etherized,
a swirling mirage, a stranger impassive,
like Lady Macbeth to madness driven.

Today I feel like staring at fire
until my eyes are burned of tears.
Today I feel like dancing on graves
until the earth opens
and swallows my pain.

TURQUOISE SKY AND WATERMELON WIND

Turquoise sky and watermelon wind
called to me in a life long past,
igniting flames of imagination
but yielding only ashes
that fell like snowflakes from above,
suffocating my dreams.

Void of seasons, never-changing,
sketching scenes of damaged hopes
and promises never meant to be,
the turquoise sky ensnared me
as watermelon winds blew sweet.
Irresistible was their allure
but cruel like stars on dirty streets
steeped in desolation.

Reflections roam throughout my mind
returning me to places where
the turquoise sky and watermelon wind
concealed the miseries, veiled the pain.
They sing to me their melancholy tune,
a melody of dreams, so long ago...
so very far away.

UNCIVILIZATION

I am lost in the celadon jungle
of your ape-man eyes.
Your tribal drums
leave me mesmerized.

The cannibal moon shines
on trembling flesh
perfumed and glistening;
nipples hard and lotus pink
beckon in the night.

Lips of lava crimson
suck deep like hungry quicksand,
drip like rainforests wet
with steam.

In our ritual dance of savage love
our bodies sway in Voodoo rhythm:
belly to belly,
mouth to mouth.

Adorned with feathers,
shells and beads,
you give your sacrificial offerings
to my volcano goddess
hot and bubbling.

In your carnal forest I surrender
like a naked butterfly
taken by the wind.
On hands and knees, I come
to you... a wild gazelle.

THE UNDEAD

In peace rests not his cursed soul
but in my bed at night he lies,
draped in fearful funeral black
against my pearly nakedness.

My looking glass bears not his image,
only rays of silver-blue light
which through my windowpane
come prowling
like beasts that hungrily hunt the night.

Warm and sweet, my scarlet nectar
from his bearded mouth does trickle,
staining sheets of ivory lace
with pinwheels red and glistening.

My heart for him alone does beat;
my quivering flesh
at his command.

In silent passion bittersweet
he tastes my life
and drinks me dry.

THE UNFINISHED NOVEL

Upon the writer's desk it sits,
an unfinished novel, its paper
blank and dusty; hungry for
words to give it closure.

Passed down from one
generation to the next, a story
of suspense and murder,
snuffing out the lives of all
who dared to write its ending.

Its pages, white like snow on
graves, allow no peace of mind.
Day and night they click away
like typewriter keys within the
writer's head; slowly spelling out
his madness.

His unfinished novel cannot
be burned or destroyed, though
time and time again he has tried,
and time and time again
he danced with failure,
scorching only his own
fingertips.

Upon his desk it sits,
a book of shadows.
It can have no final chapter,
be it joyous or one of sorrow,
whether twisted or predictable

like the anguish that arises
from the core of its mystery,
for to write its ending
is to taste death.

VICIOUS CIRCLE

In love there is desire;
In desire there is greed;
In greed there is anger;
In anger there is hate;
In hate there is war;
In war there is death;
In death there is peace;
In peace there is beauty;
In beauty there is love;
In love there is desire...
and forever the vicious circle turns.

VOW OF OBEDIENCE

"Kill her!" it demanded in a voice that sounded very much like Sister Benedicta's; only it possessed a disturbing tone of cruelty – an insatiable bloodlust driven by pure evil, if you will. "I need blood, and she needs to die. *Tonight.* There's plenty of room in the vineyard for one more girl. Don't turn away from me, bitch, when I'm speaking to you!"

Sister Benedicta's instincts told her not to look. She felt the urge to flee, to keep on running, and to never look back. But she knew it would follow her. It always did. She recalled the day when it first made its evil presence known to her. It was when she took her Vow of Obedience – the same day that her sister died in a house fire. Naturally, she had feared for her sanity in the beginning, and even considered consulting a psychiatrist or having herself committed, but she soon came to realize that the voice that sounded like hers came not from within her own mind.

It came from the deepest, darkest bowels of Hell.

She reluctantly turned her head back to look at it, as it had instructed her to do. She felt compelled to obey its commands, no matter how diabolical they were. Her stomach swam with queasiness as she made eye contact with it... a face she had come to fear. A face that was but her own reflection in the old mirror that hung on the wall in her cold and sparsely furnished sleeping quarters.

"But, I can't do it," the dark-haired nun whimpered softly to her reflected image. Tears welled up in her dark brown eyes. "Please. Not anymore. I just can't."

"You must!" the voice that sounded like hers insisted. Its tone had become even more vicious than before. It reverberated inside the nun's head, instilling within her a sensation of vertigo.

"But, she's like a daughter to me. So young... so very innocent," the disconcerted nun pleaded, while trying to maintain her balance. Her hands and lower lip trembled. She knew that her words were in vain; but, nevertheless, clung to a shred of hope that her reflection in the mirror would be merciful this time.

It was not.

"I don't care one bit about that!" the voice that sounded like hers hissed. "If you choose to disobey me, I'll burn down this convent. And everyone in it, including you, will die. You know I can make it happen, and there's not a fucking thing you can do to stop me."

Sister Benedicta picked up the large wooden crucifix that sat atop her small, beat-up chest-of-drawers beneath the mirror and tenderly caressed it, hoping to garner some comfort from it. "I realize that," she said, tearfully. "I won't disobey you. I swear."

"Good," commended the voice that sounded like hers. "Then you must carry out your dark deed tonight... and you must kill that girl in the same way that you exterminated the other three. Did I ever tell you how delicious they were? Oh, stop your sobbing, Benedicta. You should be used to killing by now."

"I'm not," declared Sister Benedicta. "I will never get used to ending innocent lives and draining their blood for you. It's wrong. It's sinful! You've made me break one of God's Ten Commandments: Thou shalt not kill. You've corrupted my soul."

"Enough of that bullshit!" angrily barked the voice that sounded like hers. "I don't want to hear anymore of this! I need human blood to sustain me. Warm, sweet, fresh human blood. And, like it or not, you are the chosen one to do my bidding."

The nun's mirrored image displayed a look of hunger. The pupils of her eyes dilated, turning the irises almost completely black. Her lips grew a deep shade of scarlet-red and stretched into a frightening, demonic grin.

Sister Benedicta shut her eyes. She could no longer bear to gaze upon her own reflection in the mirror. She gripped the crucifix and then began to pray out loud. "Almighty God, I have sinned against you, through my own fault, in thought, and word, and deed."

"Stop that praying!" the voice that sounded like hers screamed inside her head. It then growled like a dog. Vicious. Rabid. And then it snorted like a sow. "I'm warning you!"

The mirror began to rattle and soon the lower half of its wooden frame pulled away from the wall, as if by invisible hands, and then violently slammed back against it. It pulled away and slammed again and again; each time, causing a grenade of excruciating pain to detonate inside the praying nun's head.

"Heavenly Father," Sister Benedicta continued, ignoring the pain and defying the demonic voice and the contorted face that glared at her from the reflective surface of the mirror. "I ask that you hear my prayer and grant me forgiveness of all my sins. I ask that you grant me the grace and comfort of the Holy Spirit." She then opened her eyes and swung the crucifix at the mirror with all of her might as she cried out, "Amen!"

With a loud smashing sound, the mirror's glass shattered into thirteen jagged pieces, some of which landed on top of the chest-of-drawers, and some of which landed on the floor. A sudden cold wind rushed through the room and then it was gone.

Sister Benedicta smiled and felt enraptured. She was sure that the demon that willed her to kill had been cast out and no longer exerted any control over her body, mind and soul. She felt in her heart that God had truly answered her prayer and delivered her from evil. She was free, at last.

All at once, she experienced a great tightness in her chest, similar to a fist clenching. She dropped the crucifix, which broke in two upon hitting the floor, and clutched at the left side of her chest with both hands in a feeble attempt to quell the intense pain. She began to stagger like a drunk, knocking into the chest-of-drawers and stepping upon some of the pieces of shattered glass. Her eyes filled with panic. She struggled to call out to God, but her mouth was unable to form words. As a cold sweat poured out of her skin and a feeling of impending doom overpowered her, she let out a loud, horrible gasp and then collapsed onto the floor – dead from cardiac arrest.

The gruesome discovery of Sister Benedicta's discolored and bloated corpse was made the following morning. Sister Maria and Sister Agnes had been sent to check up on the nun when she failed to appear for breakfast, and were horrified to find her lifeless body on the floor when they entered her room.

From the thirteen pieces of the broken mirror, Sister Maria's reflection peered up at her, wearing a strange grin that unsettled her. Goosebumps sprung up along her arms. Without knowing why, she was suddenly overwhelmed by the urge to pick up one of the shards of glass and slash Sister Agnes' throat with it. And then a voice that sounded very much like her own, only cruel and bloodthirsty, whispered inside her head, "Kill her!"

THE END

WALK ON THE MOON

I'll take you high,
I'll take you far;
on wings we'll fly beyond the stars.
Love is within and shining
like a fiery Phoenix,
like a gold unicorn.
Distant worlds are rising;
together we can be reborn.

Infinity is in your soul
like a doorway to a cosmic hole.
You can climb into a different time
and let the universe inside your mind.
Just look and you will find.

Walk on the moon,
expand your mind.
Dance to the tune of space and time.

I see your eyes are burning
like an ancient temple to the god
of the sun.
The wheels of time are turning;
soon we'll be as one.

Let me take you to a different plane.
If you let me, I will heal your pain.

THE WEEPING RAIN

And the weeping rain falls silently down
upon this night of purple velvet;
daunting silence you wear like a crown;
at stroke of twelve it chimes spellbound
and restless ghosts from their graves arise
to once again haunt me with anguished eyes.

And the time stands still as meaningless words
engraved upon a window frozen;
melt and drip like a wound oozing blood
upon my pillow stained with mud
from dreams of graves and wedding gowns
as weeping rain falls silently down.

"SHE IS NOT DEAD
BUT SLEEPETH"

WHEN ONLY WORDS REMAIN

Someday you'll read this but I will be gone;
a pensive poem only will remain.
My words like earthbound snowflakes in the air
shall touch your eyes and quickly melt away.

Someday you'll read this and perhaps you'll laugh
at each wrenching tear that I've shed in vain…
each one an author of my epitaph;
perhaps you'll weep or maybe feel my pain.

Someday you'll read this but I'll not be there;
reclaimed, devoured by the earth I'll be.
The pages of my books shall turn to dust
and time shall fade me from your memory.

Someday you'll read this, many years from now;
you'll think me but an echo from the past…
a sad refrain, a morbid melody,
like wilted flowers in an urn of brass.

WHITE DOVE

White dove, pale as the morning mist,
and fair as the maiden whose lips once kissed;
a child of magic, cloaked in night…
into the starlit sky take flight.

And soar beyond the slumbering dells,
follow the woods and sacred wells
to shadowed hills where legend tells
of wondrous wizards and their spells.

White dove, take me on your wings
when tolls the bell with thirteen rings.
Upon the four winds we shall glide;
I give to you my heart to guide.

A WIND SO BITTER

The wind of November blows bitter and cruel
against my pane and through my brain,
preventing me from forgetting
a year has come and gone.
How strange to remember the hospital smells
within this different space and time.
Was all of it an illusion?
Or is today the dream?

And through the glass I gaze and reflect
November the thirteenth, it took you from me.

Time is a liar; its promise to heal
is broken with each passing day.
With teardrops sweet I curse it,
one more wish; a wish in vain.
This wind of November relentlessly taunts,
I see your eyes, a frozen stare.
Do you watch my crying?
Your tears have come and gone.

Haunted by phantoms, regretting cruel words,
razor sharp to cut the pain.
Will death be our reunion?
Or merely end self-loathing?
The wind of November alone only knows
the secret it will never tell,
and yet it blows so bitter
against my shuttered pane.

And from this place I should move on

but November thirteenth won't set me free.

Gray thoughts and ashes are all I have left
but comfort neither one can give.
To hasten my forgetting,
into the wind I scatter.
Oh how I hate this cursed month,
the barren trees and bleak, bleak sky.
Each year they will remind me that
your lips will smile no more.

THE WIND WHISPERS "GYPSY"

The wind whispers "Gypsy"
as she prowls the moonlit streets.
A huntress of the night,
she wears her dreams like charms.

Her hair is black as midnight
when starless is the sky;
her silhouette, cat-like,
speaks to me in riddles.

In a magic circle she slumbers
when rays of sunlight stream,
dreaming guarded dreams,
casting spells elusive.

The wind whispers "Gypsy"
as her eyes of emerald shine.
The deeper into them I gaze,
more secrets there are to find.

WIZARDBORN

Child of the stars,
you were born in a wizard's dream
on a morning trapped in
parallel time.

Space traveler, lost in the solar wind,
somewhere in another life
we will meet again and be as one.

Eyes of space magic,
like distant constellations
in the chameleon sky,
they will haunt me forever.

WOMAN OF THE WOODS

In great white feathers
she comes, wearing horns,
naked as the woods in winter.

Hair like a garden of wild ebony
weaves a tapestry, magical
as she kneels down to draw
her circle in the black flesh
of the damp earth.

Daughter of Diana
when shadows swallow the day
she lights a fire dream-bright
on her hill of emerald blades
that sway lazily in the breeze.

Huntress of the dark,
she moves with grace and speed,
fast as lightning, bold as thunder.

From Wolf Moon to Cold Moon,
living natural and free
like a tribal woman-child
of the great Earth Mother.

2000

Starcraft engines ignite
laser beam dreams
of Owsley white.

Incessant universe;
into her azure eyes
we dive, floating free.

Star-speckled highways
beckon, leading us
to the outer limits
of the human mind...

A new world
to be reborn in.

LURID LIMERICKS

43 Verses About Murderers, Monsters and Maniacs

Miss Madeline's marriage is stellar
To blissfulness love does propel her
  The secret she said
  Was to wealthily wed
And then dig a grave in the cellar.

* * *

A cannibal chef from Peru
Came down with a case of the flu
  He stayed home in bed
  With a warm human head
That he plucked from his leftover stew.

* * *

A man found himself out of luck
When one day squashed flat by a truck
   Quite an error was made
   When to rest he was laid
Because premature burials suck.

There was an odd farmer named Ed
Who fancied the flesh of the dead
  For a mask he did crave
  So he dug up her grave
And removed his mum's face from her head.

* * *

There once was a murdering nurse
Who wrote of her dark deeds in verse
  Like a psychotic poet
  But her patients didn't know it
Until they wound up in a hearse!

* * *

In London a mystery madman arrived
From butchering women his pleasure derived
  Equipped with a scalpel
  He crept through Whitechapel
And nary a one of his victims survived.

* * *

In Fall River none did confess
To who made the blood-splattered mess
　　Which through the house spread
　　Staining everything red
And much to the housemaid's distress.

The Blood Countess known as Bathory
Took pleasure from murder most gory
  A true psychopath
  She loved a blood bath
In fact she was quite predatory.

* * *

A railway conductor named Savage
Discovered a corpse in the baggage
  The smell was not pleasing
  To stop him from wheezing
He let it off at the next bridge.

* * *

There once was a fellow named Vlad
A love for impalement he had
  He told wondrous tales
  Of his victims' entrails
Until he went totally mad.

* * *

Beware of the man with black gloves
For strangling is all that he loves
  In alleyways dark
  He hunts like a shark
But chokes up when push comes to shove.

There once was an innocent teen
Possessed by a demon so mean
  She made a rude sound
  As her head spun around
And ejected a gusher of green.

* * *

A gent by the name of Mad Jack
Was seen with a large burlap sack
  In the graveyard he lurked
  And when caught he just smirked
That his job was a pain in the back.

* * *

A man with a strange savoir faire
Unleashed a horrendous nightmare
  With a Beatles LP
  He went on a death spree
But he kept it a Family affair.

* * *

The mincemeat in Grandmother's pie
Is flavored with arsenic and lye
  At weddings, communions
  And family reunions
They say for a slice they could die.

A freeloading oaf dared to crash
Count Dracula's Halloween bash
  By the end of the night
  He had perished from fright
And his carcass wound up in the trash.

* * *

When full is the moon he does howl
And through the woods on all fours prowl
  So keep in your room
  A wolfsbane in bloom
Or your innards he might disembowel.

* * *

In everyone's closet you'll find
A skeleton of every kind
  For one real go-getter
  The more bones the better
So he dug up the graveyard and dined.

* * *

Beware of our dear nanny's wrath
Her mind's on a dangerous path
  Like the rest you'll be found
  To have suddenly drowned
When she gives you your afternoon bath.

There was a young lady named Minnie
Who traveled abroad to New Guinea
  She offered a bribe
  To a cannibal tribe
But they shunned her for she was too skinny.

* * *

There once was a sensuous witch
Whose hair was the color of pitch
  She sneaked from her coven
  To go join a love-in
Where more than her nose did she twitch.

* * *

A mutated creature from hell
Below in the sewer did dwell
  His eyes flashed like lasers
  His fangs slashed like razors
But more monstrous still was his smell.

* * *

A black widow named Betty Jean
Was on husband number thirteen
  She kept getting married
  To men who got buried
With hardly a break in between.

There was a mad doctor named Frank
Who used the spare parts from a tank
  For his monstrous creation
  Which flattened the nation
And rose to a General's rank.

* * *

Young Damian asked his dear mother
Why he had no sister or brother
  She then did recall
  That he murdered them all
And that's why there was not another.

* * *

The children on All Hallows' Eve
Avoid the abode of Big Steve
  He thinks it quite dandy
  To eat them like candy
Leaving their parents to grieve.

* * *

The shop class of Wilford the teacher
Was prized for its specialty feature
  But alas he was caught
  When his students were taught
The assembly of Frankenstein's creature.

An oddity from Seminole
Who was born with the face of a mole
  Traveled only at night
  For his looks were a fright
And by sunrise returned to his hole.

* * *

With words that imparted great dread
Wanda the sorceress said
  I'm fresh out of mandrake
  So you'll have to just take
Your coffee with creamer instead.

* * *

Igor thought it would be cool
To be a professional ghoul
  He dug up a stiff
  But gagged with one whiff
And dropped out of grave-robbing school.

* * *

Young Edgar was fond of Marie
To propose, he got down on one knee
  But to his great dismay
  She just faded away
For a ghost of a chance had not he.

A frank undertaker named Fred
Of basketball players once said
  To fit them in coffins
  We must all too often
Use loppers to take off their heads.

* * *

A bumbling Satanic high priest
Attempted to raise up the Beast
  He got a surprise
  When nothing did rise
So he threw in a packet of yeast.

* * *

A smiling clown lived a sad life
With plenty of sorrow and strife
  By chance he discovered
  That happiness hovered
Soon after he chopped up his wife.

* * *

A glum suicidal arranged
To put her head in a gas range
    She first should have checked it
    For the stove was electric
So her plans at the last minute changed.

The BTK killer once said
That murder went straight to his head
  He used not a gun
  For that was no fun
He preferred strangulation instead.

* * *

There once was a lass named Aileen
Who found shooting men to be keen
  At her state execution
  She swore retribution
But that will remain to be seen.

* * *

There once was a freckle-faced teen
Whose hair had a bloody red sheen.
  Her gun shot eleven
  Which felt just like Heaven
For Mondays just weren't her scene.

* * *

Boris, a daft evildoer
Attempted to dump down the sewer
 A dead hooker's head
 But he fell in instead.
Shaking his fist, he said, "Screw her!"

A serial killer named Duff
Committed his crimes in the buff
 When strapped to Old Sparky
 He said rather snarky
This seat on my bare bum is rough!

* * *

Mortimer Dowd was a creep
Through windows at night he did peep
 He made the mistake
 Of peeping Big Jake
And wound up in several heaps.

* * *

There once was a man named Lamar
Whose habits were rather bizarre
 He liked to play coroner
 And dissect a foreigner
And keep all their brains in a jar.

Marie Antionette lost her head
And unsympathetically said,
"Let them eat cake" –
 Her first big mistake
She should have said 'strychnine' instead.

About the Author

Born and raised in the Chicago area, Gerri R. Gray is a novelist, a poet with a dark soul, a cemetery photographer, and a lifelong aficionado of horror, dark humor, and camp. She blames her twisted sense of humor on a wayward adolescence influenced by the likes of Monty Python, Charles Addams, Frank Zappa, and John Waters.

Her interest in writing started early on in life, and she began writing poetry, music, short stories, and plays while a teenager in the 1970s. Her first notable publication occurred in October of 1976 and was an interview the she and her cousin conducted with Ides of March singer/songwriter, Jim Peterik (who went on to find even greater success with the rock group, Survivor.) Her poetry has appeared in a number of literary journals and anthologies.

In 1980 she founded a small publishing company called, Golden Isis Press, and did double duty as editor and publisher of *Golden Isis Magazine* until its discontinuation in the early 1990s. Writing under a pen name inspired by an H.P. Lovecraft novel, she began a successful career as an occult author in the late 1980s and, over the course of two decades, had over two-dozen books on various New Age subjects published by

Citadel Press, Penguin, New Page Books and Adams Media.

Gerri's non-fiction article, "The House of Many Shadows", appeared in Lynda Lee Macken's book, *Ghost Hunting the Mohawk Valley* (Black Cat Press, 2012). It chronicled the paranormal activity and investigations which took place at the historic 19th century mansion in Upstate New York that the Grays currently live in, and out of which they operated a bed and breakfast themed after the 1960's supernatural daytime drama, Dark Shadows.

She has also contributed to HellBound Books anthologies, *Beautiful Tragedies* (compiled and edited by Xtina Marie), and *Demons, Devils & Denizens of Hell: Volume 2* (compiled and edited by P. Mattern).

For more information, please visit Gerri's website at:
http://gerrigray.webs.com/

Follow her on Facebook at:
https://www.facebook.com/AuthorGerriGray/

Amazon author page: https://www.amazon.com/Gerri-R-Gray/e/B076GTZ8XK

HellBound Books author page:
http://hellboundbookspublishing.com/authorpage_gray.html

Other titles from HellBound Books for your delectation…

The Amnesia Girl

Filled with copious amounts of black humor, Gerri R. Gray's first published novel is an offbeat adventure story that could be described as One Flew over the Cuckoo's Nest meets Thelma and Louise.

Flashback to 1974. Farika is a lovely young woman who wakes up one day to find herself a patient in a bizarre New York City psychiatric asylum. She has no idea who she is, and possesses no memories of where she came from nor how she got there.

Fearing for her life after being attacked by a berserk girl with over one hundred personalities and a vicious nurse with sadistic intentions, the frightened amnesiac teams up with an audacious lesbian with a comically unbalanced mind, and together they attempt a daring escape.

But little do they know that a long strange journey into an even more insane world filled with a multitude of perilous predicaments and off-kilter individuals are waiting for them on the outside. Farika's weird reality crumbles when she finally discovers who, and what, she really is!

Beautiful Tragedies

Only through dark poetry can a tragedy become something truly beautiful.

"Beauty is in the eye of the beholder." This phrase has origins dating back to ancient Greece, circa 300 BC; proving that some humans have always had the ability to see beauty where others could not.

Beautiful Tragedies is a compilation of 140 works by no less than fifty-five amazing poets writing in a variety of forms--all inspired by feelings born in the darkest of times.

They express the pain associated with unrequited or all-consuming love gone wrong, as well as where the resulting emotions can take us. Readers will get in touch with the darkness lurking inside all of us—the ugly part of us—where we can consider the unthinkable, stemming from the madness gripping our minds.

Detours and Dead Ends

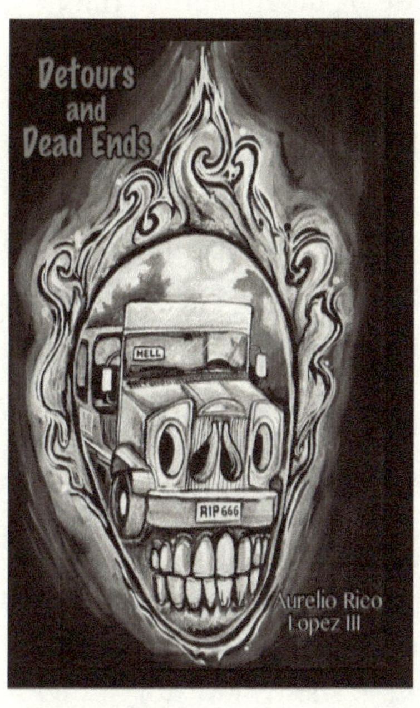

There are so many poems that invoke feelings of romance, wonderment, and joy.

These aren't them.

Aurelio Rico Lopez III is an exceedingly talented writer and poet who manages to conjure up scenes of mayhem, fear, and cosmic dread in this poetry collection, Detours and Dead Ends.

Lopez brings a bit of artistic flare to his signature style of writing and provides a book that takes the reader from murder to revenge, from unfortunate circumstances to several different flavors of the apocalypse.

So crack it open and enjoy the ride..

<u>Tripping Balls</u>

A thought provoking, eclectic, disturbing and at times downright weird collection of poetry, short stories and insightful musings from the inimitable Gocni Schindler....

He offers a variety of stories which beautifully gives the awesome reader, like you, the opportunity to experience different levels of thought and contemplation. I know, it's so exciting! God willing, some humor as well.

The book takes off with a top shelf short story titled Hell-A-Expense. Super! Within this tale, the Demon takes possession of its victim and takes you along for the ride as a co-conspirator. Don't do anything I wouldn't do! Step right up, step right up! Meet Johnny B Fast and the tale of Dynamic Drunken Disorderly. Damn, that's a memory! Moving along, moving along,

Oh, yes, we stop at the tale of Henrietta and her treacherous trip. What a bitch! Insane is sexual. Oh, look, another fine telling of a good story! Mental Blues and a possible moment at the mental ward. 'Innocent I tell you, I'm innocent!' Stop right there! Let me introduce you to the Homeless man, Ronin, and that good buddy Actor Man and yes, there is an almighty telling of their rotten tales.

Dark Musings

The perfect companion piece to Light Musings – The dark side of Xtina Marie's poetry delves into intense emotions: heartache, loss, hurt, pain, rage, and a dangerous consuming love which can drive one insane. Dark Musings is not a collection!

The author returned to the centuries old practice of Narrative Poetry—the telling of a story through poetry. If you believe you are brave enough to explore the savage emotions of the human heart; Dark Musings will test your mettle.

Light Musings

The perfect companion piece to Dark Musings – an intriguing mirror image of the darkness you have just read, but no less deep and soul stirring.

What a web she weaves. Light Musings is a poetic narrative—a story told through related poems. Xtina Marie is a master of this style. Known by her fans as the Dark Poet Princess, this term of endearment came about as a result of the horror genre embracing her first book: Dark Musings which continues to garner stellar reviews. Light Musings will not disappoint her loyal fans as darkness is present within these pages as well. However, this latest book will show a much larger audience that Xtina's poetry pulls out every feeling the reader has ever experienced—forcing them to feel with her protagonist. Light Musings shows us that love is made from darkness and light; something Xtina Marie explores like no one else.

**A HellBound Books LLC
Publication**

www.hellboundbookspublishing.com

Printed in the United States of America